Never Look Back

································

Judy Baer

BETHANY HOUSE PUBLISHERS
MINNEAPOLIS, MINNESOTA 55438

Never Look Back
Copyright © 1997
Judy Baer

Cover illustration by Chris Ellison

Published by Bethany House Publishers
A Ministry of Bethany Fellowship, Inc.
11300 Hampshire Avenue South
Minneapolis, Minnesota 55438

Printed in the United States of America.

Library of Congress Cataloging-in-Publication Data

CIP Data applied for

ISBN 1–55661–837–9   CIP

Never Look Back

Cedar River Daydreams

9708

For Deborah Gulbro Stave

JUDY BAER received a B.A. in English and Education from Concordia College in Moorhead, Minnesota. She has had over forty novels published and is a member of the National Romance Writers of America, the Society of Children's Book Writers, and the National Federation of Press Women.

Two of her novels, *Adrienne* and *Paige*, have been prizewinning bestsellers for Bethany House. Both books have been awarded first place for juvenile fiction in the National Federation of Press Women's communications contest.

Chapter One

The Hamburger Shack was filled with the usual after-school crowd. Lexi Leighton and Todd Winston were the first to arrive at their regular table. Lexi's thick hair tumbled over her shoulders, and she pulled it away from her face with a familiar gesture.

"I am *so* glad today is over. I thought I'd never get through that presentation in class. My topic was so boring, *I* almost fell asleep giving it." Lexi scanned the menu out of force of habit, although she always ordered French fries and shared a banana split with Todd.

"I thought it was pretty good," Todd said, his dark blue eyes twinkling and the tiny dimple in his cheek growing deeper. "Of course, I couldn't hear all of it over the snoring in the class."

"Very funny." Lexi didn't take offense. Instead, she waved to Jennifer Golden and Peggy Madison as they made their way to the table. "Wait until it's your turn. I'll bring a pillow."

Peggy was grinning as she walked toward them.

Her thick red hair was pulled back in a barrette. Freckles were scattered across the bridge of her short nose. Jennifer, on the other hand, was trying her best to look bored with the energy in the room. A tall blonde with bright blue eyes and an athletic build, Jennifer chomped on a wad of chewing gum, snapping it noisily as she dodged tables and boys blowing the paper covers off straws.

"We have got to find a better place to meet," she announced when she reached Lexi and Todd. "This place has lost all its class."

"It never had any class, Jennifer." Jerry Randall appeared next to her with an order pad in hand. "So what do you want?"

Jerry was dark haired, handsome, and cocky. He'd worked at the Hamburger Shack for as long as Lexi had lived in Cedar River. He lived with his aunt and uncle while his parents worked as engineers for an oil company in the Persian Gulf.

"Something without grease or calories," Jennifer retorted.

"Then you've come to the wrong place." Jerry turned to Lexi. "The usual?"

Lexi and Todd nodded together. While Jerry was taking Jennifer's and Peggy's orders, Egg and Binky McNaughton weaved their way to the table.

Brother and sister, the McNaughtons were hard to miss no matter *how* large the crowd. Binky was tiny and quick. Because her eyes were pale and her hair an ordinary reddish brown, Lexi often thought of her friend as a little bird—petite and plain but full of attitude. Her brother, Egg, was a larger version of Binky, but another bird altogether. He was part stork and part flamingo, with his long neck, large Adam's apple, and quick blush, which could turn him pink at a moment's notice. A lanky bean pole of a guy, Egg was all elbows, knees, and heart. The McNaughtons were two of Lexi's favorite people in Cedar River.

"Tim and Anna Marie had to stay after class to take a test they missed," Binky announced breathlessly as she threw herself into a chair. "Matt said he was going to Mike's garage to work on his bike. Egg told Angela we were coming here, but I don't know where she is."

"Then that accounts for everyone," Jerry said, referring to the group of friends who usually hung out together. "Except for Angela. Is she coming?"

"I thought she was absent today," Peggy said. "At least, I didn't *see* her."

"She's been absent a lot lately. Isn't she feeling well?" Jennifer asked as she reached for a handful of napkins.

"I asked her that," Lexi said. "She said she was fine, but she didn't explain why she's been missing school."

They all looked at Egg for an explanation.

"I don't know. Maybe she's busy."

"Okay, okay," Jerry said impatiently. "Now, will you hurry up and order?"

Just as Jerry was leaving the table, he was accosted by another group, this one made up of several girls. Each was well dressed and wore flawless makeup, expensive book bags, and bossy expressions.

"Aren't you going to wait on us?" one of the girls asked.

"Let me put in their order first," Jerry said, referring to Lexi's table, but Minda Hannaford caught him by the sleeve.

"Not till we order. Right, girls?"

Tressa and Gina Williams and Rita Leonard all nodded. Jerry gave a helpless shrug and started taking orders.

"Can you believe the nerve of them?" Binky fumed. "We ordered first, and now they'll probably get their food before us."

"So what's new? The Hi-Fives have been cutting us out for as long as I can remember. Why should they stop now?" Peggy sounded resigned.

"At least they haven't added anyone new to their little 'club' lately," Jennifer pointed out. "Maybe people are catching on that they aren't as cool as they think they are."

The Hi-Fives recruited members for their group and demanded unwavering loyalty to the clique. Lexi had once been one of those recruits but was thankful it hadn't worked out.

"Did you see the football game last night?" Todd asked Jennifer, who was a fan.

"How about that touchdown right at the end? Was that cool or what?" Jennifer and Todd started a spirited conversation that lasted until their food came.

Egg plucked nervously at his French fries. "I wonder where Angela is. Do you think she forgot I told her we were going to be here?"

"Don't worry, Egg. She just walked in." Todd pointed to the door with his spoon. Everyone turned to watch Angela move toward them.

Jennifer spoke first. "What's wrong with her? She looks terrible!"

Angela did look pale. Her shoulders were drooped and her eyes were red. She dropped into the chair next to Egg with an ungraceful plop.

"You're late," Binky accused.

"Am I?" Angela seemed uninterested in the fact. When Jerry came to take her order, she waved him away.

"Not hungry?" Egg looked worried. With his unfillable stomach, lack of hunger and lack of health went hand in hand.

Angela looked at him absently. "Hmmm? Oh, I'll just share yours." She took a French fry and dragged it through Egg's ketchup.

Jennifer raised her eyebrows but didn't comment.

Egg patted her on the hand. "You look nice today. I like your hair."

Peggy whistled. "Isn't that sweet?"

But Angela just stared at her hands, hardly responding to the compliment other than with a disinterested "Thanks."

Egg tried several more stabs at cheering her up but failed miserably each time. Then Peggy brought up the latest gossip about a new student teacher, and Angela's odd mood was forgotten. Egg occasionally sent a puzzled look her way, but he kept quiet.

Lexi, watching this silent exchange, was curious, too. Angela was not usually a moody girl, and Egg could almost always tease or flatter her out of the dumps. Then Lexi's attention was diverted by an eruption of voices at the Hi-Fives' table.

"I can't believe it! No way!"

"I'd be so mad if that happened to me."

"If my parents ever made me do that, I'd leave home!" That statement from Gina caught everyone's attention.

"Do what?" Jennifer asked. She was never afraid of butting into a Hi-Five conversation.

Gina turned to her, wearing an indignant expression. "Minda's mother is into 'new rules.' She can't go out on weekends until she finishes her chores. Can you believe it?"

"I've never even had chores before," Minda complained. "Mom's been going to some support group, and she's getting all these ideas."

"It's a stage," Tressa assessed. "Mothers go through them all the time. She's being unreasonable right now, but she'll get over it."

"Doesn't she realize that you're already seventeen? Next year when you're eighteen you can do whatever you want. You're practically an adult already." Gina was outraged.

"I'd leave," Rita said. "Go live with your father."

Much to the surprise of the eavesdropping table next to them, Minda didn't join in the criticism of her mother. Finally she admitted, "Maybe it is a little bit my fault that my mother's upset."

"Why?" Gina asked.

"Yeah, why?" Jennifer echoed.

Minda had the good sense to look embarrassed. "I was supposed to clean up after supper last night because Mom had a tennis lesson. I guess I forgot. Somebody called, and I decided to drive around for a while. They came to pick me up, and I must have been in a hurry because I didn't close the kitchen door very well."

"Not putting away leftovers and leaving a door open got you in trouble?" Gina asked.

"Sort of. We have a lot of dogs in our neighborhood. Two Old English Sheepdogs, a German shepherd, and a pair of golden Labs. A couple of them must have smelled the food and nosed their way into the house."

"Uh-oh," Rita muttered.

"They kind of, like, broke some dishes and dragged a pan of barbecued ribs onto the carpet. When Mom came home, one of them was sleeping on her bed."

"Maybe I wouldn't move out just yet," Rita backtracked. "Sounds like you aren't quite ready to live on your own. What if the dogs had gotten into *your* room? Gross!"

The Hi-Fives were still discussing Minda's latest problem as they paid their bill and left the Shack. The kids at Lexi's table waited until the door had closed behind them to burst into laughter.

"Can you believe it?" Peggy asked, horrified. "If I'd done that, I'd be paying for new carpet!"

"And Rita's telling her to move out? Minda still needs a caretaker!" Binky said.

"Or a zoo keeper," Egg muttered.

Everyone laughed at that except Angela. She didn't even seem to have heard Egg's little joke. Her expression told her friends that her thoughts were a million miles away.

———

"My stomach hurts," Binky whined the next day as they entered their classroom. "I hate speech class. It makes me so *nervous*."

"You'll do fine. You talk all the time and don't seem nervous," Lexi pointed out.

"That's what Egg says. What does he know? Maybe I won't get picked to speak today." Then Binky groaned. "And if I don't, I'll have to be nervous even longer!"

As it turned out, Tim Anders was the first to give his persuasive speech entitled, "Why Fathers Do Know Best."

"My dad has been getting smarter and smarter," Tim began. "Why, his intellectual growth is positively amazing. When I was thirteen and fourteen, I thought my dad knew absolutely nothing. But the older *I* get, the smarter *he* gets."

Tim went on, cleverly letting the class know that it was he, Tim, who had been the one lacking wisdom, and only now was he beginning to really appreciate the things his father knew. With example after example of times his father had known best, Tim drove home the point that teenagers would be wise to listen to their parents. Though he had the entire class laughing, his conclusion was serious.

"I know that parents can be a real pain with all their rules and lectures and that I-know-what's-best-for-you attitude, but the more I mature, the more I realize that they often *do* know what's best. They were kids once, too. They made mistakes. But all parents want to do is keep their children from hurting themselves or being hurt. So if Mom or Dad is getting on your nerves, rather than tuning them out, tune them *in*. They might be smarter than you think!"

Everyone clapped enthusiastically—especially Binky. Lexi had a hunch that she was doing everything in her power to drag out the class and avoid giving her speech for another day. Lexi knew she had guessed right by the big sigh of relief Binky gave when Matt Windsor's name was called next.

Matt was dressed up for the occasion, Lexi noticed. His black hair was pulled back into a tight ponytail, exposing the shaved lower portion of his head. He wore a discreet gold earring and a black chamois shirt with faded jeans.

Lexi smiled to herself. Just looking at Matt, one

would never know what a sensitive, serious thinker he was or how hurt he'd been when his mother left his father and took his sister to live with her in Canada. Matt had struggled to get along with his new stepmother and all the drastic changes in his life.

"My topic is 'Emancipated Minors,'" he began. "They are teenagers who are legally free to live alone."

Lexi noticed Angela sit a little straighter in her chair, lean forward, and show interest for the first time that hour. As Matt explained the reasons and the legalities of such a situation, Angela began to scribble notes in the margins of her notebook.

"Comments anyone?" Mrs. Thompson asked when Matt had finished. "Do you notice anything interesting going on here?"

"Tim tried to persuade us to listen to our parents, and Matt advocated living independently of a parent's control," Jennifer offered. "They were promoting opposite ideas about parents."

"Very good. I'm delighted that it worked out this way," the teacher said. "Because now you as students will have an opportunity to decide which speech was more persuasive and why."

Tim and Matt both looked unhappy at the prospect of having their speeches so closely examined but didn't have time to dwell on it since it was Angela's turn to speak.

She moved hesitantly toward the front of the room, her nervousness apparent in every step she took. She placed her note cards on the podium, took a deep breath, and addressed the class.

"Homeless. Do you know anyone who is or has been homeless? Without anywhere to go or any address at which to receive a letter? Can you even imagine being in such a predicament? Afraid of sleeping in the cold? Hungry, and not sure where your next meal is coming from? Dirty, and no sink or shower in which to wash up? Well, I can imagine it—because I've *lived* it!"

Lexi could see several students in the class shifting uncomfortably. Although she and the rest of the gang had known about Angela's past for a long time, not everyone in school knew of the circumstances of her life before Cedar River. Lexi glanced at the topic list for the speeches to be given. Angela's was entitled "Why People Should Support Missions and Shelters for the Homeless."

Angela's nervousness evaporated as her passion for her topic swelled within her. She talked about the weeks that she and her mother had lived in Cedar River's mission and of the kind people who took them in, gave her mother a job, and helped them to get the apartment where they now lived.

"How did we make it? Sometimes I still wonder," Angela continued. "But we scraped by. My mother and I were a real team then. We were there for each other. I might not have had a home, but I had love."

Suddenly, her eyes filled with tears. Angela drew her fist to her mouth as if to press back a sob. Almost before anyone realized what was happening, she gathered her notes and raced out of the room without finishing her speech.

The uncomfortable shifting of some of the students broke the quiet. Lexi raised her hand. "Should I go after her?" she asked.

"That would be a good idea," the teacher said. "But give her a few moments to compose herself." Then, refocusing the students to the task at hand, she began giving out assignments.

As soon as the bell rang, Lexi jumped to her feet, gathered Angela's books, and raced to find her. Angela was not in the bathroom, nor was she anywhere in the vicinity of her locker. Lexi checked the *Cedar River Review* room, the gymnasium, even the faculty rest rooms. Angela was nowhere to be found.

"Have you seen her?" Lexi asked as Egg and Binky exchanged books in their lockers.

"No . . . do you think she's all right?" Egg looked as though he was going to burst into tears, too.

"She'll be okay," Lexi said soothingly, although she wasn't sure she believed her own words. "I've just got to figure out where she went."

"Tell her to call me?" Egg pleaded.

"Of course."

Lexi continued her search until she had to go to math class. *Maybe that's where Angela has been all along*, Lexi thought. She took a deep breath and tried to reassure herself. Maybe they'd just missed each other in the crowded hallways.

But Angela wasn't there, either. Lexi had no

choice but to slip into her desk under the disapproving glare of the teacher.

"Have any of you seen Miss Hardy?" Their math instructor was eyeing Angela's empty desk.

The students shook their heads, confused.

"Miss Hardy has missed three classes this week. If any of you see her, I suggest that you tell her I would like her to come see me. Soon."

While everyone else turned to their assignments, Lexi sat stoically, attempting to keep her lip from quivering and her legs from shaking. Angela was in big trouble now. Her teachers were growing angry with her behavior. Her friends were confused. It was as though their friend was changing right before their eyes.

Chapter Two

"I'm not done with my assignment," Jerry Randall hissed into Lexi's ear. "How about you?"

"You need to ask?" Jennifer muttered. "Lexi is *always* done with her assignments."

"Oh yeah. I almost forgot." Jerry turned away as Lexi shot Jennifer a scowl.

Usually she *was* prompt with her homework, but last night she'd had a hard time studying. Angela had been on her mind all evening.

Though Lexi had looked for her again after school and called the apartment, she hadn't found her friend. In fact, she hadn't seen her at all until this morning when Angela slunk into the school, head down, eyes averted, looking as if she didn't want to talk to Lexi or anyone else. She had even brushed Egg off at the lockers, and he was still moping about it.

Her first chance to get close to Angela was in English class, where they were assigned to small groups for a discussion on *Huckleberry Finn*.

Todd had already picked up the list of questions

each group was to consider, and Jerry had put four desks in a circle when Lexi and Angela joined them.

Angela looked terrible. Her face was pale, and dark circles smudged her face beneath her eyes. Her hair, usually combed and attractive, had been pulled away from her face in a hasty ponytail.

Lexi put out a hand and laid it on Angela's wrist. "Are you okay? I looked for you after speech class yesterday, but I couldn't find you."

"I had to get away for a while, that's all," Angela said softly. "I shouldn't have chosen that topic for my speech. It made me too emotional."

"It was great," Lexi told her. " Mrs. Thompson said so, even though you didn't finish it. You'll have to give her the rest later. I think you'll get an A."

"It wasn't worth it," Angela muttered. She opened her book and stared at the pages, clearly indicating the conversation was over.

Jerry made a face over the top of Angela's head and signaled to Lexi to be quiet. Lexi glared at him but said nothing. Maybe Jerry was right. Perhaps the best thing to do was to leave Angela alone for a while.

Todd picked up the question list and read the first line. " 'Why is Huckleberry Finn the most famous runaway of all time?' " He scratched his head. "I don't know."

"Probably because he's the one runaway everyone has read about," Lexi suggested. "Mark Twain had been a popular author for years. Huck Finn and Tom Sawyer are practically folk heroes."

"Besides," Jerry added, "who knows a lot of runaways *other* than them? It's not like the people who run away from home publicize it a lot."

"True," Todd said. "But there's something else wrong with this picture."

Angela gave a grunt of agreement but didn't speak.

"What do you mean?" Lexi hurried to fill in the awkward silence following Angela's response.

"Huck Finn's story isn't very typical. After all, he spent his time with Jim going down the river. I doubt most runaways have the fun Huck had, but they do have the troubles."

The discussion in the group grew lively, but Angela, Lexi noticed, seemed distracted. She sat slumped back in her chair, her jean-clad legs stretched out in front of her, her hands folded over her books. Occasionally she made a small sound of agreement or disagreement. Other than that, it was as if she wasn't there. When the bell rang and small-group leaders handed in their papers, she left without a word to anyone.

———————

"Will you eat with me, Lexi?" Ben asked. "I'm making peanut butter crackers and milk."

"You're cooking? Sure. Just so I don't have to do it myself."

"Are you tired?" Ben asked with concern as he put the crackers out on the counter and arranged them in a pile.

"You could say that. I had a weird day at school."
Even though she couldn't explain to Ben about Angela's strange behavior, Lexi knew she had a sympathetic ear in her little brother. Every fiber of Ben's body was sweet and compassionate.

Ben took the peanut butter from the shelf and methodically began spreading it not only on the crackers but the counter as well. "*I* had a good day."

"Then why don't you tell me about yours." Lexi took two glasses from the cupboard and milk from the refrigerator. She sat at the end of the counter and took the smeared crackers Ben pushed her way.

"I played kickball." Ben grinned widely. "I'm good."

Lexi returned the smile. "I'll bet you are." She thought about how cool it was that Ben was so proud. Having Down's syndrome wasn't a problem at the Academy for the Handicapped where Ben attended school. They encouraged him to be the best at everything he could do.

"I think you're a jock," Lexi mused. "One of those athletes that girls like to watch."

A giggle erupted from Ben, and he hid his face in the crook of his elbow. When he surfaced, his cheeks were pink. His almond-shaped eyes twinkled merrily. In a low voice he confided, "I gots a girlfriend. We're in like."

"Huh?" Lexi wrinkled her nose. "What's that?"

"We're in *like*!" he said again. "Teacher says we're too little to be in love, but we're never too little to be in like."

Lexi burst out laughing and came around the counter to give her brother a squeeze. "Benjamin, that's the funniest thing I've heard in ages!"

Ben looked pleased with himself. "I know."

"What's going on in here?" Mrs. Leighton walked into the kitchen carrying a paint brush in one hand and a canvas in the other.

"Ben's telling me about his new girlfriend," Lexi said.

"Another one?" Mrs. Leighton ruffled Ben's hair. "Too much charm. That's your problem."

"Want a cracker?" Ben asked, bored with the girlfriend conversation.

"No thanks. No treats for me until I get this painting finished. I'm under a tight schedule."

"What's the hurry?" Lexi asked.

"I'm feeling good these days," Mrs. Leighton said, referring to the off and on condition of her multiple sclerosis. "I want to get as much done as possible. The gallery has been begging me to do another show, and I'd like to finish enough pieces so I can accept."

"Are you sure you're up to it?" Lexi voiced her concern. Her mother had suffered some bad times.

"Absolutely. My book is finished and making the rounds of publishers. I have to keep busy or I'll be a nervous wreck wondering if someone will take it."

"That book means a lot to you, doesn't it, Mom?"

"Very much. When I was diagnosed with MS, I saw the need for a book for children that would explain why Mom or Dad is sick. I still think it's important. If someone publishes my book and it helps only a handful of kids, that will still be enough."

"Since everyone else has so much going on around here, I guess I'd better get busy, too," Lexi said.

"What are you going to do?"

"I'm going to cut blocks for a quilt I'm planning to make."

"Didn't you just finish a quilt?" her mother asked.

"This one isn't for me. Last time I visited Grandma at the nursing home, the social director said they were trying to earn money to buy tickets to local theater productions so that the residents could attend. I told her I'd make a quilt to be auctioned off at their fund-raiser."

"How nice of you, Lexi."

"It should be easy," Lexi said. "I'm going to have each of my friends decorate a block in any way they want. Then I'll sew the blocks together. It should be cool."

"What a wonderful idea! May *I* do a block?" Lexi's mother asked.

"You'd like to?"

"Sure, it will be a nice break from the big canvasses I'm working on. I'll do something small. The drawing can be transferred easily to cloth."

"Me too!" Ben cried, his face covered with peanut butter.

"Wow! This is great. I'll cut your blocks right

away. What are you going to use to decorate your block, Ben?"

"My pets." Ben leaned over to let his dog, Wiggles, lick his fingers.

Lexi wiped her hands and headed for the dining room, where she removed the lace tablecloth from the table and spread out her sewing gear. It felt wonderful to plunge her hands into the soft, cottony fabric and admire the bright, crisp colors. Her friends often teased her about the time she spent sewing, but Lexi always smiled and said sewing was her stress reliever. And today, after Angela's puzzling behavior, Lexi especially needed the concentration sewing demanded.

She was nearly through cutting blocks with her big yellow rotary cutter, the one Ben called her "pizza cutter," when Lexi's mother entered the room.

"You should see what's going on in the backyard," Mrs. Leighton said, laughter filling her voice. "Ben's trying to get the dog and the rabbit to pose for him so he can draw them. I suggested taking a photo of them first, but he seems to think this is the way 'real' artists work."

"You do it," Lexi pointed out.

"Yes, but my still life subjects usually *are* still—fruit, flowers, trees."

"Oh well, it will keep him busy for a while." Lexi laid the cutter on the large green mat in the center of the table and dropped into a nearby chair. "I can hardly wait to start sewing this quilt together. It's going to be fun."

Mrs. Leighton sat down across from her daughter. "From the expression on your face, I wouldn't guess it would be any fun at all. You look very somber, dear."

"That doesn't have anything to do with the quilt."

"Want to talk about it?"

"I don't know what to say. Angela Hardy has been acting weird lately, that's all." Lexi told her mother about speech class and how Angela had run out of the room, then not showed up for her next class.

"Have you talked to her about it?"

"No. I'd like to, but I doubt I could even get a few minutes alone with Angela these days. She's keeping everyone at arm's length. It's obvious she doesn't *want* to talk to me—or to anyone."

"That's a problem, then," Mrs. Leighton agreed. "If she's not ready to talk about what's bothering her, all you can do is let her know you'll be there for her when she is ready."

Lexi nodded morosely. That was the hard part—waiting. Then she sat a little straighter in her chair. Just because Angela wasn't talking didn't mean *all* of her friends would be closemouthed.

She jumped to her feet and plucked some quilt blocks from the pile she'd cut. "I'm going to deliver these," she said to her mother. "Be back in an hour."

There was someone she needed to see.

———

Every light was on in the McNaughtons' well-worn house. A fat, lazy tomcat slept on a denim jacket on the top step by the front door.

Lexi didn't bother to knock but just stepped inside and called out, "Anyone home?" She could hear music playing upstairs and then the sound of footsteps and muted conversation.

"Is someone down there?" a female voice asked.

"I didn't hear anything," a male voice responded.

"Turn down the music!"

"This is my favorite song."

"Binky! Egg! It's me, Lexi!" she hollered at the top of her lungs. The music faded, and she could hear two sets of footsteps pounding down the stairs.

"I *told* you someone was here," Binky chided.

"It's no big deal. It's just Lexi." Then Egg blushed. "I didn't mean that like it sounded. I just meant—"

"Never mind," Lexi smiled. "I know what you were saying, and I'm glad I'm considered family at your house." Lexi winked at both of them. "And I didn't know you have a new cat."

Binky and Egg stared at each other. "What cat?"

"The one sleeping on your jacket on the front steps."

"So that's where my jacket went!" Egg yelped.

"It must be the neighbor's cat," Binky deduced. "At least I don't *think* we got any new pets."

Before the McNaughtons could get into one of their bizarre family discussions—like who owned the cat—Lexi held out the quilt blocks she was carrying. "Here, I brought these for you."

"Scraps of cloth. Thanks, Lexi, but you shouldn't have." Egg didn't look impressed.

"They're quilt blocks. I'm asking each of my friends to decorate one. Then I'll sew them together and donate the quilt to the nursing home to be auctioned off as part of a fund-raiser."

"Cool." Binky took a piece of fabric. "What do I do with it?"

"Anything you want. Draw on it with pen or paints. Embroider a design. Sew on lace or buttons or anything that would make it pretty."

"And what about me? I can't do any of that," Egg complained.

"Then it's probably time you learned," his sister retorted unsympathetically. "I'll help you."

That, Lexi thought, *is going to be like the blind leading the blind, since Binky is no more artistic than Egg.* Still, Binky always came through in a pinch, and this would be no different. Lexi had confidence that whatever the McNaughtons came up with, it would be one of a kind.

"Todd is drawing a picture of his old car," Lexi told him, referring to Todd's 1949 Ford coupe, his pride and joy. "Then his mom is going to do counted cross-stitch over it. It will be great."

"What is Peggy doing?" Binky asked.

"Making a shape with buttons and yarn."

"Is *everyone* doing this?"

"I'm asking all my friends," Lexi said.

"What about Angela?" Egg's question had a double meaning, and Lexi knew it. He hadn't seen any more of her than the rest of them.

"I've got a quilt block for her, too, but I haven't given it to her yet."

"I see." Egg glanced at the floor. "When you see her, say hi from me."

"Can't you say it yourself?"

"I don't know anymore. She hasn't wanted to talk to me much lately."

"Do you know what's bothering her?" Lexi asked.

Egg looked as though he didn't want to have this conversation. Then he gave a resigned little sigh. "Sort of. She's told me a few things, but I don't know if she wants it spread around."

Lexi put her hand on Egg's arm. "Don't tell us if it means breaking your word to her, Egg."

"Oh, I didn't promise anything. I just . . ." His voice drifted off and he looked pensive. "She probably wouldn't mind you knowing anyway. She practically talked about it in speech class to everyone."

Egg sat down at the kitchen table and signaled for the girls to join him. "Angela is unhappy because she and her mother aren't getting along."

Lexi and Binky were both surprised.

"I can't believe it," Lexi murmured. "Angela and her mom are too close for that. It's been just the two of them for so many years."

"They're best friends! She even told the class that she and her mom were a team," Binky exclaimed.

"I know," Egg agreed. "The operative word there was 'were.' She and her mom *were* a team, but they aren't anymore. All of Angela's life, she and her mother have been alone together. I've never heard Angela say a bad word about her mom. They've depended on each other for so long that Angela can't imagine being without her."

"But Mrs. Hardy isn't going anywhere!" Binky protested. "This doesn't make any sense!"

"Remember the guy that came to pick up Angela's mom at her birthday party? I think his name is Ted Smith. Well, they've been dating for a while now. She met him through someone she works with. Apparently Angela's mom really likes him." Egg chewed on his lower lip with an air of frustrated concentration. "*Really* likes him. According to Angela, her mom and Ted have gotten very close."

New understanding glimmered in Binky's eyes. "And now Angela's jealous!"

Of course, Lexi thought. Why hadn't she remembered her brief conversation with Angela about this very subject until now? Suddenly things were beginning to fall into place.

Egg frowned at his sister. "You make it sound so crummy, like Angela is being petty or selfish. You know she's not like that!"

"I understand what Binky's saying, Egg," Lexi said. "But I'm sure she doesn't mean Angela is selfish. If I were Angela, I'd be *scared*."

Egg looked puzzled, as if that thought had never occurred to him. "Scared?"

"Sure. My mom and I are plenty close, but we've never had the kinds of experiences that Angela and Mrs. Hardy have had. If Mom was all I had and some man came along and started taking up all the time that had once been for me, I'd be terrified."

"So Angela is afraid of losing her mom to this guy!"

Lexi nodded solemnly. It hadn't occurred to her until just now how serious Angela's problem might be. "It makes sense now, doesn't it?"

"Too much sense," Egg agreed sadly. "I feel so sorry for her. Her life must feel like it's upside down."

"How unfair!" Binky protested. "Angela's had enough bad times. Why is her mother doing this to her?"

Both Lexi and Egg stared at Binky, who flushed and cleared her throat. "I mean . . . well, I guess . . . oh, all right! I suppose it's natural for Mrs. Hardy to want someone her own age around to talk to, but can't she see what it's doing to Angela?"

"Angela is good at hiding her feelings," Egg said as he stared at his feet. "Maybe her mother doesn't realize how much this bothers her. Besides, Binky, you know how *you* act when Harry's around."

Harry was Binky's sometimes boyfriend who'd gone away to college. When he was home, Binky tended to have eyes only for him.

The threesome visited a few more minutes, mostly about the quilt blocks Lexi had brought. Then Lexi excused herself and said good-bye. She was thoughtful as she walked down the McNaughtons' driveway. It only took her a few seconds to make a decision. Instead of turning toward home, she started out for Angela's place.

———

The Hardys' apartment was one of many in a nondescript row of brick buildings. Lexi walked slowly up the stairs, taking deep breaths and praying silently, "I'm nervous, Lord. Help me to say the right thing to Angela. Help me to help *her*."

Angela came to the door after Lexi's third knock.

"What are you doing here?" was her ungracious greeting.

"May I come in?"

"Sure." Angela stepped out of the way and beckoned Lexi into the spotlessly clean apartment.

"Are you home alone?" Lexi asked, looking around the quiet living room.

"As usual." There was bitterness in Angela's tone. Biting her lip, Angela sheepishly added, "I just mean that Mom is out quite a bit lately, that's all."

Lexi said nothing but pulled a quilt block out of her pocket.

"What's that?"

"I've started a project for my grandmother's nursing home. I'm making a quilt to be auctioned off in a fund-raiser. I thought I'd ask each of my friends to decorate a block any way they'd like. When everyone is done, I'll sew it together."

"That's nice." Angela sounded as if she hadn't even been listening.

"So you'll do it?"

"You mean you want *me* to sew?"

"You can ask your mom to help you. I'll bet she'd have some good ideas." Lexi regretted the words as soon as they left her mouth.

Angela's head snapped up, her eyes flashing. "I'm not going to ask her to help me! She's never home. She couldn't fit it into her *schedule*. Maybe you'd better have Ted ask her to do it."

Angrily, Angela stomped into the kitchen and threw open the refrigerator door. She stood there staring into it. Finally, when she'd gained some control of herself, she drew out a pitcher of orange juice and set it on the counter. "I'm sorry. I shouldn't have blown up at you, Lexi. You've got nothing to do with this. Do you want some juice?"

Lexi nodded and perched on a kitchen stool while Angela poured the juice. "I talked to Egg. I know why you don't want to ask your mother to help you. He told me about the new man in her life. I guess I'd forgotten that you'd mentioned it to me once."

Angela grimaced. She slid onto a stool across from Lexi. "Egg's got a big mouth," she said softly.

"He cares about you. And he's worried. He

doesn't want you to be hurt, but he doesn't know how to help you."

Tears formed in Angela's eyes. "Oh, Lexi, I feel so *awful*! Logically I know that my mom deserves to have friends—even a boyfriend. It's really not fair of me to be so angry. This is the first time she's ever allowed herself the luxury of going out. But the more time she spends with Ted, the less time she has for me. I feel like she doesn't even know I exist."

"Do you like your mom's boyfriend?"

"No." The word was spoken harshly.

"Your mom is with him now?" Lexi asked.

"They went out for dinner. They asked me to go along, but there's no way I'd spend an evening with *him*." Angela spit out the last word as if it were poison.

"What don't you like about him? Is he rude? Mean to your mom? To you?"

"No . . ." Angela frowned. "He's polite, I guess. Just a pain."

"How?" Lexi probed. "What does he do?"

"He's always bugging me, inviting me to come with them, looking disappointed when I don't. Where does he get off putting me on a guilt trip, anyway? He's not responsible for me! I didn't invite him into my life, so why doesn't he just butt out? Why won't he leave me and my mom alone?" Angela scrubbed the tears out of her eyes with the back of her hand.

"So you don't like him because he takes your mom away. But if he invites you along and you refuse to go, that's not exactly his fault."

"I don't want him wrecking my family," Angela said stubbornly. "Mom and I were doing just fine before he came along."

"Maybe your mom wasn't doing as fine as you thought," Lexi replied.

"What do you mean by that?" Angela looked angry.

"Maybe she was lonely and just didn't say anything to you."

"But she has me," Angela insisted.

"Think about it, Angela. You have lots of friends other than your mom, and you have Egg."

Angela's shoulders sagged, but her look remained stubborn. "You don't know what you're talking about."

Lexi forged ahead, hoping that what she was going to say wouldn't ruin her friendship with Angela. "Maybe Ted is a nicer guy than you think. After all, your mom is a great lady. She has good taste. Why would she go out with someone bad for her?"

Angela's mouth worked as she tried to formulate an answer. Finally she said, "That's not the point."

"Then what *is* the point?"

"He's changing my mother!" Angela blurted.

"How?"

"She's going out all the time. She's started to fuss about her clothes, and she's even wearing makeup! They have dinner, go to the theater . . ."

"That sounds all right to me," Lexi murmured.

"That's because it's not *your* mother. Since Ted,

everything has changed. Mom doesn't have time for me like she used to. Every night she'd cook supper. Now I'm heating pizzas or cooking for her! We used to spend time together. Now she spends her free time with Ted.

"Don't you see, Lexi? Our lives were finally settling down. For the first time Mom and I have a real home. She has a job. I have friends. Life was finally getting good, and I liked it the way it was. For once I was really happy. Then Ted came along and changed everything. I don't want things to change. Why is my mom trying to mess everything up now?"

Chapter Three

"Tomorrow we'll be having a quiz on the portion of *Huckleberry Finn* that we've covered in class."

Books started slamming shut even before the teacher was done speaking. Egg poised on the edge of his chair, ready to escape. When the bell rang, he bolted out of his seat. The others caught up to him in the hallway.

"Had a little too much caffeine today, Egg?" Jerry asked. "Or are you always this jumpy?"

"Very funny. Have you seen Angela?"

"No. Was I supposed to?"

Egg turned to Todd and Lexi. They both shook their heads.

"I don't think she's in school," Lexi said.

"We had two tests today, and she wasn't there for them," Egg blurted. "She hates to make up tests. Maybe she's really sick."

"We get out early, too," Jerry pointed out. "She'd be crazy to miss a day with only one afternoon class."

That statement only increased the worried frown lines on Egg's forehead. "Maybe I'd better stop by her apartment and see how she is."

"But if she's sick, Egg, she's probably sleeping," Lexi pointed out. "Todd and Binky are coming home with me. Why don't you come, too? We'll call Angela from there."

"Okay," Egg said doubtfully. "I suppose I'm being paranoid, but Angela's been so down lately that I worry about her."

"She's fine," Binky consoled her brother. "When you get to Lexi's, you can call and find out for yourself."

————

Mrs. Leighton met them at the door. Lexi knew immediately that something was wrong.

"Mom? What's wrong?" Lexi felt her stomach lurch. Her mother almost never met her at the door. What's more, the expression on her face told Lexi that something had happened.

"Lexi?" Binky murmured. "What's up?"

"Come inside, kids. I have something to tell you."

They trailed Mrs. Leighton into the living room and sat down. Four pairs of concerned eyes stared at Lexi's mother.

"Mrs. Hardy called this afternoon," she began.

"I knew something was wrong! I just knew it!" Egg twitched and jerked on the couch. "Angela is in the hospital, isn't she?"

"No, Egg, Angela's not sick."

"She isn't?" Egg frowned. "Then what's wrong?"

Mrs. Leighton sighed. She appeared to be choosing her words very carefully. "According to her mother, Angela was picked up by the Cedar River police this afternoon."

Egg's mouth dropped open and he stared at Mrs. Leighton, speechless.

"There must have been a mistake!" Todd finally blurted. Lexi's and Binky's heads bobbed in agreement.

"No mistake, I'm afraid. Mrs. Hardy was very upset, but from what I gather, Angela had gone to the bus station and was loitering there."

"She wouldn't do that!" Binky yelped. "That's not like Angela at all!"

"Well, she did. And since the police have had some complaints lately about transients and vandalism at that bus station, they've been patrolling it very carefully. There were some . . . questionable . . . looking people there, and when they were picked up, Angela was among them."

"So it was all a big mistake?" Egg asked with apparent relief in his voice.

"I suppose it could have been straightened out easily if Angela had cooperated, but she wouldn't. She refused to give the police her name or address. They believe she was trying to run away from home and would have succeeded if not for this incident."

"Run away?" Lexi echoed blankly.

"Why?" Todd's face was a mask of confusion. He was still unaware of Angela's problems.

"Apparently Angela and her mother have been having some trouble. On top of that, the school called to say that Angela has been skipping classes so frequently, she's dangerously close to failing some of them."

Lexi exchanged nervous glances with her friends. They all knew Angela had been erratic in her attendance, but they'd never guessed it was this serious.

"Wow!" Binky whispered in amazement. "Classes are always boring as far as I'm concerned, but I don't *skip* them."

Mrs. Leighton continued. "Angela's mother and I talked for a long time. She's very concerned. She wants to understand what's gone wrong in her relationship with Angela and why she's behaving this way. She was wondering if any of you could shed some light on the problem."

"Does she want us to go over there?" Egg asked.

"She'd appreciate it," Mrs. Leighton replied.

"Let's go right now!" Binky jumped to her feet.

"I don't get it. I just don't get it," Egg muttered again as they approached the door to the Hardys' apartment. He'd been saying that over and over as they'd driven to Angela's home. *No one* got it. That was obvious.

Lexi had a heavy feeling in the pit of her stomach. As Egg knocked on the door, Lexi remembered what Angela had told her about her feelings for Ted and her mother. Were things really so bad that Angela felt she had to run away? Surely Angela wouldn't do anything so stupid, would she?

Angela's mother answered the door. It was obvious she had been crying. Though she'd tried to hide the fact with makeup, she couldn't hide the red-eyed puffiness or the look of quiet desperation. She wearily motioned Lexi and her friends inside.

"Let's sit in the kitchen. Angela's sleeping in the back bedroom. I don't want to wake her."

"Is she okay?" Lexi asked.

"She's been crying a lot. We both have. She finally exhausted herself. I just don't understand what's going on, and I don't know where else to turn."

"Have you talked to Angela about this?" Lexi asked softly.

"Talk to her? I've tried, but lately she won't talk to *me*. It's as though my beautiful little girl has turned into this hostile, angry creature. . . ."

"She hasn't been easy for us, either," Lexi admitted. "She's changed lately, especially at school."

"We're all confused by the way she's been acting," Egg admitted. "Angela and I used to tell each other everything—at least I thought we did. But now . . ."

"What on earth is causing her to behave this way . . . even to try to run away?" Mrs. Hardy asked.

Lexi realized Angela hadn't really told her mother what she thought of Ted or how threatened she felt. Lexi didn't know what to do. She didn't feel comfortable interfering, but Mrs. Hardy should know how her daughter was feeling. And since Angela wasn't talking . . .

Lexi was about to explain to Mrs. Hardy what she knew when she saw Egg's warning glance. She bit her lip as she caught his meaning. If Angela thought her friends' confidences couldn't be trusted, she wouldn't share any more with them. Egg could be right. Maybe it wasn't wise to say too much just yet.

"This is driving me nuts!" Egg said from the Winstons' couch. His feet were waving in the air, his head touching the floor, and his back resting on the seat.

"And sitting upside down helps?" Todd carried in a tray of sodas and chips.

"I can't think right side up. I have nothing to lose by trying it out."

They'd come to Todd's place after their talk with Angela's mother, needing time to consider all that had happened.

Mrs. Winston entered the room. "You kids look miserable!" Todd's mother exclaimed. "Binky, you are white as a sheet. Are you feeling okay?"

"Not really. My stomach hurts."

"I have an antacid in the cupboard."

"It's not that kind of stomachache."

"We just feel blown away, Mom," Todd said. Then he told her about Angela.

"No wonder you're upset. That sounds very out of character for her."

There was no condemnation or judgment in Mrs. Winston's voice. Lexi appreciated that fact. It made Todd's mom much easier to talk to.

"I just don't understand it," Egg said. He swung his feet around to sit upright on the couch. "Angela isn't the kind of girl who hangs around until she gets arrested and then refuses to talk to the police! I just don't *get* it!"

"I suppose none of us does," Mrs. Winston said quietly. "After all, only Angela lives in Angela's shoes."

"I'm sure she's rebelling because she's angry with her mom," Todd said. "Maybe she's looking for ways to hurt her."

"But it's not as though her mom's done anything wrong. She's free to date if she wants to." Binky looked truly puzzled.

"I'm sure Angela knows that logically," Mrs. Winston replied. "But it's not her logic that's talking right now. It's her emotions. She's hurt, angry, and afraid. Skipping classes and hanging out in the wrong places may be her cry for help."

"I just want to know what to *do*," Egg wailed.

"Well, I think her behavior is *mean*," Binky announced.

"Mean? Why?"

"Because she's worrying all the people who care about her. She's scaring me! I think Angela is being very selfish."

"That's not nice to say—" Egg began.

Mrs. Winston stopped him. "But in a way, it is true. Angela loves her mother very deeply, and yet she's hurting *her*, too. She is confused right now and not thinking straight. She's only concerned about herself. When she is able to put her emotions into perspective, *then* she'll realize that this isn't the answer. Not before."

"You mean she might do something else this stupid?" Binky asked, horrified.

Mrs. Winston remained silent.

———

Lexi's parents were already in bed when she got home, but their reading lights were still on. Her mother often read at night, and Dr. Leighton, because he was often called to work early in the morning, liked to go to bed early.

Lexi knocked on their door and entered at their invitation.

"How is everything?" her mother asked.

"All messed up." Lexi looked at her parents. Her dad's hair was ruffled from running his fingers through it. Her mother wore hers pulled away from her face in a ponytail. They both stared back with loving eyes.

"Want to talk about it?" her dad asked.

Lexi launched herself onto the bed and gave them each a hug, clinging so tightly that Mrs. Leighton finally protested that she couldn't breathe.

"I love you guys," she said fervently. "No matter what."

"That's good to hear," Mrs. Leighton said mildly, stroking her daughter's hair. "And we love you—no matter what."

"That's what good families do, isn't it?" Lexi asked. "Love people even if they aren't perfect?"

"God loves us that way. How can we do any less for our children?" Dr. Leighton said.

Comforted, Lexi said good-night to her parents and went to bed.

Chapter Four

"It was really pretty cool," Angela said as she curled into a corner of the couch in the Leighton living room. "In a weird sort of way."

Jennifer, Lexi, and Binky stared at her in disbelief.

"Cool?" Jennifer yelped. "Getting arrested is cool?"

"It wasn't like I'd done anything illegal. I just happened to be in the wrong place at the wrong time, and the police thought I was involved with the others."

"Wrong place, all right. Why would you hang out there, anyway? And during school hours!"

Binky looked so shocked and appalled that it was hard for Lexi not to laugh even though she felt the same way. Angela was calmly sitting there, talking as though being arrested were an adventure, not a disaster!

"Tell us exactly what happened," Jennifer said. "All we know so far is that the police picked you up along with another girl."

Angela curled a little deeper into the cushions. Lexi thought she looked more nervous than she wanted to let on.

"It was no big deal, really. A mistake. Now, for Janie it was different."

"Is she the other girl?"

"Yes. She wasn't from Cedar River. She was a runaway."

"I can't imagine running away from home," Binky said. She screwed her face into a frown. "Even as much as Egg bugs me sometimes, I couldn't go."

"That's because you've got it good at home. You don't know what it's like for some people." Angela's voice trembled with emotion.

"Why did Janie run away? Did you find out?" Jennifer was curious.

"She ran away because she was sick of having to take care of her two brothers and two sisters."

"I have to take care of Egg," Binky pointed out. "He certainly can't take care of himself."

"That's not what I mean. Janie's mom died, and her dad expected her to take over all the responsibilities. He said he'd hire someone to help them but never did. Janie had to do all the cooking, cleaning, and laundry."

"Wow," was Binky's awed response. "That's terrible!"

"After a while, Janie said her friends just stopped calling her because she could never go out with them anyway. Her dad worked all the time, and when he didn't they just had big fights. She said that he was avoiding hiring help because all this work kept her at home. He didn't want her running around, and it was his way of controlling her."

"That's mean!" Now Binky was indignant. "Couldn't she talk to him about it?"

"No. He wouldn't listen. He liked it the way it was. He had a free housekeeper, and it kept her out of trouble."

"Wasn't there anyone who could help her?"

"She said she had a pretty good teacher in one class. He didn't talk down to her. He knew how hard her life was at home and he tried to give her a break. But that teacher had a heart attack and died. Janie said she felt like everyone who cared about her was dying. That's when she decided to take off. She wasn't going to let whatever was happening to her affect anyone else."

"That's dumb," Jennifer said.

"Maybe, but it's how she felt." Angela defended the girl. "Besides, nobody can understand how someone else feels."

Lexi wanted to interject that she thought otherwise, but before she could say anything, Binky piped up.

"What did Janie do then? Where did she go? Cedar River?"

"No. First she hitched to a friend's house. She stayed there a few days before she moved on. She was afraid her dad had called the police, and she didn't want anyone to find her. When she ran out of money, she got a job in a hotel as a maid. She figured that was one way to stay out of sight."

"But where did she *live*?"

Angela's expression darkened. "Anywhere she could. Then, through some kids she met, she found out there was an empty house where some other runaways were staying. She found it and asked if she could join them."

"Did they say yes?" Jennifer asked.

"They did. They all agreed to share whatever food they had. It worked out pretty well for Janie, until she got caught taking a shower in one of the hotel rooms she was supposed to be cleaning. She was fired, but she still had a place to live. The other runaways became like a family to her. Then her dad found her. He was really angry, too, because after she ran away he had to take care of the other kids himself. It cost him a bunch of money to pay someone for what Janie had done for free. He brought her home. She stayed for a week and ran away again. She was just passing through Cedar River when the police picked her up. Bad luck, huh?"

Lexi frowned. "It seems like Janie and her father could have worked something out."

"Why? All he did was use her. She was like a live-in nanny and housekeeper—a slave! Nothing she said helped. It just got to be too much for her, that's all. Her father should have known he was asking too much. Parents are supposed to *see* when they're hurting their children!" Angela's voice rose a notch. It was obvious that she was thinking of her relationship with her own mother. "Parents are supposed to be on their kids' side, aren't they? Parents aren't supposed to be selfish."

"Parents are human, too," Lexi pointed out. "I'm not sure having kids guarantees that you'll be perfect. Maybe just more tired."

"That's what my mother says," Binky agreed. "She says Egg and I make her *very* tired!"

"Well, I don't blame Janie," Angela mumbled. "I just wish she hadn't gotten caught. If the Cedar River police hadn't been alerted, neither of us would have gotten into any trouble."

"What will happen to her now?" Binky wondered.

"She'll probably get sent home again."

They all sat quietly, thinking about what Angela had said. Sending Janie home wasn't going to fix the problem. It would just be a matter of time before she ran again.

———

A few days later, Lexi poked her head into her mother's studio. Mrs. Leighton was studying a still life of vegetables and flowers she'd arranged.

"Do you think another potato would improve the balance?" Mrs. Leighton touched a tulip with the tip of her brush.

"Looks good to me. I can't believe potatoes, onions, lettuce, and tulips look good together, but they do."

"I wanted to do something fun. If it doesn't turn

out the way I want, I'll hang it in the kitchen."
Lexi's mother turned to her. "What are you up to?"

"I thought I'd go over to Angela's and see how
she's doing on her quilt square. I'd like to start sewing them together soon. I'm afraid I'm going to have
to do some nagging with everyone in order for me
to finish up."

"Let me guess," Mrs. Leighton said with a
laugh. "Egg and Binky are making a huge project
out of this. Something with sequins and lights."

"Close." Lexi smiled. "Nothing Binky and Egg
ever do is easy. I think they actually *like* chaos. And
speaking of chaos, I'd better get over to Angela's.
Her life is pretty mixed up, too."

Mrs. Leighton nodded distractedly. She'd already returned her attention to her painting.

Lexi smiled to herself as she thought about her
mother. When she was painting, she could block out
the world. Lexi was usually like that at the sewing
machine. But recently, Angela's problems and erratic behavior had interfered with just about everything.

Lexi rang the doorbell of the Hardy apartment.
She was surprised when a tall, handsome man
opened the door.

"Come in," he invited as he stepped aside.

Angela's mother was sitting at the kitchen table, her hands wrapped around a coffee mug. A second mug, still steaming, sat on the other side of the

table. Lexi sensed she'd interrupted a very private conversation.

"I'm sorry . . . I came to see Angela. . . ." Lexi found herself stammering with embarrassment.

"Come in, Lexi. Have a chair. I'll tell Angela you're here." Mrs. Hardy rose and disappeared into the back of the apartment.

"Hi, Lexi. I'm Ted. I've heard all about you." The man gave her a friendly smile and held out his hand.

Lexi took it. His grip was firm and warm, and his eyes twinkled. She liked him immediately. "I've heard about you, too. . . ." Her words trailed away.

That was the wrong thing to say, she realized. What she'd heard about Ted was from Angela—and it was all negative. According to her friend's description, Ted could have been a fire-breathing dragon instead of a pleasant, good-looking man around the same age as Lexi's father.

Mrs. Hardy reentered the room. This time Lexi noticed that she looked very pretty. She was dressed up to go out. Unfortunately, her attractiveness was marred by the tense expression on her face.

"What's wrong?" Ted picked up on her agitation.

"Angela, of course." Mrs. Hardy turned to Lexi. "My daughter hasn't stepped out of her room since Ted arrived over an hour ago. As you know, she's having a hard time with our friendship." She looked at Ted ruefully, and Lexi could see the affectionate look they exchanged. "But it's something Angela is going to have to work through. And I just have to be patient."

Lexi willed herself to blend in with the furniture, speaking as little as possible, praying Angela would hurry. It wasn't long until the older couple seemed to forget Lexi was even there.

Ted's hand slipped across the table to cover Mrs. Hardy's, and Lexi smiled. It was the sort of thing her parents would do when they thought she and Ben weren't watching.

"It's more comfortable in the living room," Ted finally commented. "Lexi, do you want to join us?"

She didn't have much choice. What was taking Angela so long, anyway? They moved to the other room. Lexi took a chair; the adults, the couch. Ted put his arm around Angela's mother, and she curled into the crook of his arm. As they visited, they gave each other loving looks. Once, when a stray lock of hair fell into Mrs. Hardy's eye, Ted moved it gently away with the tip of his finger.

If she were any judge of happy relationships, and Lexi did have her own parents to serve as examples, Ted and Angela's mother were in love. They were thoughtful, considerate of each other, tender, gentle; all the things that her own mom and dad valued so much. They laughed easily together, appeared to think the other was full of brilliant ideas, and generally bloomed in each other's company.

But, Lexi thought, *it's one thing seeing it in your own parents or even with your friends, but it must be entirely different to see your mother falling in love.*

It occurred to Lexi that teenagers never thought much about their parents having lives of their own. They were all teenagers once, she knew, but it was almost impossible to imagine her mom and dad dating. The idea kind of turned her stomach, actually. Parents were supposed to be *parents*, weren't they?

But that wasn't fair, Lexi's logical side told her. Angela's father had been out of their lives for years and years. He'd abandoned them when Angela was a baby. Maybe Angela's mom had never really *had* the opportunity to be happy. Why should she be denied that now?

It was hard to figure out. Impossible, really. And Angela was stuck right in the middle—loving her mom and not wanting things to change, yet knowing her mom deserved friendship and happiness, too. What a problem!

"Sorry Angela is so slow, Lexi. She said she'd be out as soon as she was ready. I suppose she's really waiting for Ted to leave, but—"

"Why don't we have a soda?" Ted suggested.

"Good idea." Mrs. Hardy jumped to her feet and headed for the fridge. "Ginger ale or Coke?"

Lexi noticed how eager Mrs. Hardy was to please Ted. *That must really get on Angela's nerves if she is jealous of him already*, Lexi thought. Lexi was beginning to feel absolutely miserable.

"Ted, I don't have to work this weekend," Mrs. Hardy was saying. "And I'd love to get this apartment painted. What do you think?"

"I can help you Saturday. Do you have the paint?"

"I'll pick some up. Maybe you'd like to help me look at colors. I'd like to go a little darker in my bedroom—just to match my new spread. We'll have to look for something for Angela's room, too. Her walls really need to be freshened up—"

"I'll pick out my own paint, thank you." Angela stood in the doorway looking furious. "And I'll plan my own weekend."

"Of course, dear, we were just talking. . . ."

"You were just planning my life for me. I'd really appreciate being consulted before you make plans for me. Besides, I thought we were going to do the painting *together*."

"Don't be so hard on your mother, Angela," Ted murmured, his voice tense. Lexi could see he was trying to be patient, but the look of hurt on Mrs. Hardy's face had hurt him, too.

Angela spun toward him, her face a mask of fury. "Will you just butt out of our lives? You can't tell me what to do! You aren't my father, and I don't want you to pretend to be. My mom and I had a good life before she met you. You're ruining everything."

"Angela Hardy, you apologize right now!" Mrs. Hardy spun into action. "Apologize to Ted for those hateful words."

"No. I meant every one of them. Don't you see, Mom? We were happy the way we were. Now you spend your time looking at him with goo-goo eyes.

'Yes, Ted.' 'Sure, Ted.' 'Anything you want, Ted.' It makes me sick to my stomach."

"Don't talk to your mother that way!" Ted looked both upset and angry.

"And don't talk to *me* that way!" Angela shouted back. *"You're* the intruder here, not me! You aren't part of us!"

"Angela, stop it!"

Both Angela and her mother were crying now. Angela took her mother's arm and shook it. "Don't you see? We were happy. We were a team. Now he's in the way. Can't we have it like it used to be?"

"We were homeless and alone, Angela."

"We had each other."

"We still do, honey."

Angela glared at Ted. "Not if he's in the picture, we don't."

Lexi had been backing toward the door, eager to get away. This was dreadful. She had to get out. Everyone had forgotten she was there.

She reached the door and opened it just as the voices reached a new, even higher pitch. She escaped into the hall and covered her ears with her hands. Still, she could hear every hurtful, painful word that was said.

———

Mrs. Leighton was in the kitchen when Lexi burst through the door. "Sweetheart! What's wrong?" Mrs. Leighton was immediately on her feet.

The whole dreadful, sordid story came pouring out of Lexi.

Mrs. Leighton listened without interrupting, and her expression grew more and more sad as Lexi spoke. When Lexi was done, she said, "Those poor, poor people. How they must be suffering!"

"It was so awful, Mom. Everyone was so upset, and I didn't blame any of them! Angela's mom and Ted make a good couple. He's very nice. You can tell he cares about them both, but Angela can't see any of it."

Mrs. Leighton drew Lexi close. "Angela grew up believing that her mother was all she had. No home. No father. No brothers or sisters. Not even a pet. Only her mother. It's no wonder she's frightened. She feels her entire support system is disintegrating. Your friend feels alone and betrayed."

"It's a good thing I met Ted and saw for myself how fond he is of Angela's mom," Lexi murmured thoughtfully. "I'd have a hard time seeing you with another man even if I didn't remember ever having a dad." She shuddered. "Even *imagining* you dating is creepy."

"Angela's mother is free to date, Lexi. She's doing nothing wrong. Besides, you said Ted was a very nice man."

"But Angela said—"

"You are forgetting something," Mrs. Leighton stopped her. "Angela's mom has been alone for a long time. She needs companionship, too. Would you ask me to give up my friends so that you could keep me for yourself?"

"No, but—"

"Should I ask you to spend all your extra time with me? How would it feel if I grew jealous and possessive of *your* friends?"

"That's silly! It's not like that for the Hardys."

"Then how is it, Lexi?"

"Angela just wants her mother to be there for her?"

"And isn't she?"

"Not all the time."

"How much time does Angela spend with her mother?" Mrs. Leighton asked.

"After school, Sundays, times she's not with us," Lexi replied.

"And what should her mother be doing while Angela is busy? Just wait?"

Lexi's shoulders sagged. "I see what you mean."

"Does she ignore Angela when Ted is around?"

"Not that I can tell. Angela ignores *them*."

Mrs. Leighton nodded sadly. "This is something Angela will have to come to grips with, Lexi. What will she do if her mother decides to marry Ted?"

"Oh boy," Lexi breathed. "I don't even want to think about *that*."

But for the rest of the evening, Lexi could think of nothing else. Even when she crawled into bed that night, she couldn't help but worry over Angela's dilemma. Suppose Mrs. Hardy *did* marry Ted? Where would that leave Angela then?

Chapter Five

Lexi hummed at herself in the mirror as she curled her hair. She'd woken early and had taken time for an extra-long shower. She was enjoying the leisurely pace of the morning. She tipped her head over to shake out the cooling curls when a small voice asked, "What are you doing?"

Lexi flipped herself upright and met the stare of her little brother. "Hi, Ben. I didn't hear you come in."

"What *are* you doing?"

"Fixing my hair."

"Upside down?"

"Just shaking out the curls." Lexi arranged her hair in the mirror. "Fluffing it up a bit."

"You look fluffy enough."

Lexi laughed as she applied a second coat of lip gloss and dusted her cheeks with a pale bronzer. Lexi usually wore very little makeup, but since she'd had extra time today it was fun to do something different.

"Why do you draw on your face?" Ben wondered.

He'd perched on the toilet seat and was studying her with disconcerting intensity.

"It's not drawing, Ben. It's makeup. And I don't have to do it. I just wanted to look a little more special today . . . prettier."

Ben's brow furrowed as he frowned. "I like you just the way you are."

"Benjamin, you are such a little sweetie!" She gathered her brother into her arms, and he squealed and squirmed to get away.

"You didn't get that stuff on me, did you?" he said suspiciously, scrubbing away the kiss Lexi had planted on his cheek.

"No, I didn't. Worrywart. And why aren't you getting ready for school?"

"We don't have school this morning. My teacher has a . . . a . . ."

"Conference?" Lexi finished for him.

"Yeah. That. So I'm going to go to work with Dad. He said I could."

"Fun. You'll like that."

"I know. I like the animals." Ben had his father's affection for furry creatures. Perhaps if things had been different for Ben, he would have been a veterinarian like his dad.

"Have you had breakfast yet?"

"Nope. Mom said to wait for you." Ben grinned and hopped off the closed toilet seat.

"Then we'd better get going. *One* of us has to go to school."

———

"So then Ben said . . ." Lexi was describing to Tim Anders her morning with her brother when she saw Binky walking down the hall. She laid a hand on Tim's arm. "Excuse me. I've got to say something to Binky. Talk to you later?" And before Tim had time to answer, Lexi hurried away.

She caught up with Binky just outside the *Cedar River Review* room. "What's wrong?" Binky had obviously been crying.

"I've been looking for you! Where have you been?" Binky snuffled and dabbed at her nose with a soggy tissue.

"School doesn't start for fifteen minutes yet. I'm not exactly late. Now, will you please explain what's wrong?"

"In here." Binky pushed Lexi into the *Review* room where most of them were on the staff of the school paper.

Lexi was surprised to see that the room was not empty. Todd, Peggy, Matt, and Jennifer were seated around one of the large work tables. They stared at Lexi and Binky bleakly as the pair entered.

"You look as if there's been a death in the family," Lexi joked, then a sickening sensation in her stomach stopped her cold. "There hasn't been—is everyone okay?"

"Angela has run away," Jennifer said softly. She blinked away tears.

"No way! There's got to be a mistake. I mean,

how do you all know this? You know some of the ru-
mors Minda and the Hi-Fives have started. . . ."

"She left a note for Egg on our front door," Binky
said. "Dad found it when he went out to get the
newspaper. She must have left it there during the
night."

"What did it say?" Lexi sank into the nearest
chair, stunned by the news.

"That she wanted Egg and all her other friends
to know she was leaving. She said she was sorry,
but she just couldn't take it here anymore. She
wrote that her mom had totally changed and wasn't
the same person she used to be. Angela said she figured her mother wouldn't even miss her now that
she had Ted to spend her time with. She said she
didn't think her mother thought very much about
her anyway."

"That's not true!" Lexi protested.

"You know that, and I know that. But apparently *Angela* doesn't know it. She said there had
been a big fight."

Lexi winced. She knew about that.

"Afterward, Angela heard Ted tell Mrs. Hardy
that she was too easy on Angela, and she should
come down harder on her when she was acting up."

"Ouch," Lexi said.

"Angela said there was no way she was going to
let this guy Ted decide how her mother should behave toward her. She said she'd lived most of her
life without a father, and she didn't want one now."

"So that was it?" Lexi asked.

"Isn't it enough? This whole thing is a *disaster*," Jennifer stated. "Now Angela's gone, and no one knows where she is."

"I really can't see why she did it," Todd mused. "Why didn't she stay and work it out?"

"That's probably what you would have done," Peggy pointed out. "But Angela is an entirely different person. She's vulnerable and emotional."

"Bad choice," Todd said. "Really bad."

"She's not thinking straight," Matt said. "She feels betrayed. I've been there. I was a little like Angela when my mom left my dad and me. Someone I'd thought I could count on disappeared from my life. For a long time, I thought that if I'd been different . . . better, more obedient . . . Mom would have stayed.

"Then my dad decided to remarry. He was a lot like Angela's mom, I'll bet. Goofy. Grinning all the time. Buying new clothes for his dates and spending time on the phone." Matt shuddered. "Yuck. It isn't pretty to see your parents doing that." Then a smile split Matt's handsome features. "Then I realized that Dad wasn't even forty years old. It may seem old to us, but it's not, really."

"And you didn't care if he dated anymore?"

"Oh, I cared, all right. I felt abandoned by everyone. That's why I understand Angela. She and her mom promised that they'd be there for each other, and they were—until Ted came along. Even if Mrs. Hardy *did* try to include Angela, I know Angela thinks all her mom cares about is Ted."

"So she took off so she didn't have to watch her mother with someone else," Todd mused.

"Exactly."

"I'll bet Angela didn't even get to know what Ted is really like," Peggy speculated. "She probably hoped he'd move on if she was rude to him."

"But that didn't work," Binky concluded. "And since she had herself boxed in a corner, she left."

"Where is the note?" Lexi wondered.

"Egg's got it."

"Then where is Egg?"

"In the school office. The police wanted to talk to him." Binky's lip trembled.

"The police?" Lexi was receiving one blow after another.

"My dad said we should take the note to school and give it to the people in the office because they'd know what to do. They called Mrs. Hardy and the police. And now they're giving Egg the third degree!" Binky threw her hands into the air dramatically.

"Settle down, Binky," Jennifer growled. "They aren't shining a light into Egg's eyes to make him talk. They just want to find out what he knows about Angela."

Even the mild criticism was too much for Binky. Her small face crumpled and she began to cry.

Jennifer gave Binky a quick hug. They sat in silence, wondering if they would ever see Angela again.

"Excuse me." The policewoman cleared her throat.

Lexi's head snapped up, her thoughts interrupted at the sight of the officer. No one moved.

Todd was the first to speak. "Can we help you?"

The woman was brisk and no-nonsense in her crisp navy police uniform and dark shoes. There was an intimidating leather gun holster on her hip and a gleaming badge pinned to a shirt pocket. Though it was obvious she meant business, there was a compassionate, friendly look in her eyes.

"Did any of the rest of you talk with Angela Hardy last evening? Egg McNaughton spoke to her by phone. How about anyone else?" She looked expectantly around the room. Five heads shook in the negative.

Lexi's voice nearly failed her as she said, "I did."

"Could you come with me to the office, please?" the woman asked kindly. "Your principal has given all of you excused absences from class, so there's no need to worry about that."

"Do we just stay here?" Jennifer asked.

"Yes. Someone is on the way down to speak with you. Then you are free to return to class." She turned to Lexi. "Follow me."

Lexi's feet felt like lead as she followed the policewoman to the administration offices. A million questions raced through her brain. Why, Angela? Why? Things might be bad at home, but not so bad as this!

There was another police officer in the principal's office, this one a tall, slender young man with a thick shock of brown hair that was trying its best to be unruly underneath the official-looking hat.

Lexi wrung her hands with nervousness, wondering if anything she could say would help them find her friend.

The tall officer escorted Lexi into the conference room. It was a large room with a vast table surrounded by fifteen or twenty chairs. There was a coffee pot and stack of Styrofoam cups on a rolling kitchen cart nearby. She'd been in this room before with Mrs. Waverly but had never been here as the center of this much attention.

"Sit down, Miss Leighton," the policewoman said kindly. "No need to stand."

"Lexi. My name is Lexi." She felt a lump the size of one of Ben's toy balls forming in her throat.

"Okay, Lexi," the man said. "I'm Officer Truman, and this is Officer Bendle. We'd like to know about your last encounter with Angela Hardy. What time did you see her?" He had a pen poised over a note pad and was waiting expectantly for Lexi to answer.

After Officer Bendle had brought her a cup of water, Lexi managed to tell them what she knew about Angela and her situation. Both police officers listened attentively. Officer Truman jotted down a few notes.

When it was apparent that Lexi had told them

all she could, Officer Bendle leaned back in her chair to study her. Her expression was grave but her eyes were kind. "Do *you* have any questions?"

"Will you find her?" Lexi was shocked at how much her voice quavered. "Will Angela be okay?"

"We'll do our best," Officer Truman said.

"Officer Truman is new to our police force," Officer Bendle said. "He's just come from New York, where he specialized in cases like this."

"Really?" Lexi sat up a little straighter, for the first time feeling a little hope. "What did you do?"

Officer Bendle stood up and moved toward the door. "Excuse me, but I'll be making some calls while you two are talking."

After she left, Officer Truman leaned forward on his elbows and smiled at Lexi. "I was in a runaway unit for the city. It's a specially trained squad of plainclothes officers."

"There are that many kids to arrest?" Lexi gasped.

"There are enough runaways to warrant a special unit, but we don't arrest them. Instead, we spend our time on the lookout for kids who have been reported as runaways by their parents."

"Isn't that difficult?" Lexi wanted to know.

"Yes, it is. If your parents were to describe you, they'd say how tall you were, what color eyes and hair you had, et cetera. There would be thousands of girls who'd fit that description. Even with a photograph, it's not easy."

"If you find someone—like Angela—what do you do?"

"Try not to scare her, for one thing. We've been trained to talk to young people. We call their parents and give them the status of their child's condition. We tell them if we believe the boy or girl needs medical attention. Then we arrange to see that the young runaway gets home." He gave Lexi a gentle smile. "Sometimes I feed them. Kids on the run don't eat very well, and the first thing to do is buy them a good meal."

Lexi nodded. This made sense. She hoped that someone like Officer Truman would find Angela.

"How exactly do you look for runaways?"

"Well, New York City is very different from Cedar River. Hundreds of kids run away to New York thinking they'll make their way there. It doesn't take long for them to realize that it's not as easy as they think.

"I always worked in street clothes in New York," Officer Truman continued, "because we didn't want to alert kids to the fact that I or my partner was a cop. We either walked the streets or drove around in an old car—not a police car."

"Just looking for runaways?"

"Yes. We spent a lot of time at the bus station because kids who come from a distance usually can't afford an airline ticket. Hitchhikers are more difficult to pick up because they can be dropped off anywhere."

"Then you confront them?"

"No. Not if they aren't doing anything wrong. I can ask someone, however, about their purpose for coming to the city."

"But how do you pick them out?" Lexi wanted to know.

"That's the sad part. They're the lonely, lost-looking ones."

———————

"Is there *anything* we can do?" Lexi leaned her elbows against the wide expanse of Pastor Lake's desk. She had stopped by the church on her way home from school. After her discussion with the police, she felt the need to get more involved.

Pastor Lake leaned back in his chair and tapped the tip of his pen against the top of his knuckle. "The police are experienced in these sorts of things, Lexi. We'll have to trust them. And there's always prayer."

"I know. I mean that I'd like to . . . take *action*. Go look for her myself. Make a safe place she could come to. Be there for her and for other runaways."

Pastor Lake looked thoughtful. "Actually, you might be on to something, Lexi. Will, the mission director, and I have been discussing a runaway hotline for the mission. It would be an 800 number that runaways could call to ask for help, leave messages for their families, or whatever else they might need. But one of our primary problems right now is money. Financing the line takes money, and you know that neither churches nor missions usually have excesses of that."

"I have some in savings," Lexi offered.

"I'm not asking for your money!" Pastor Lake assured her. "Although it's very generous of you to offer. I was thinking more along the line of ideas. We'll need to do a fund-raiser."

"I'll make another quilt!"

"A quilt?"

Lexi eagerly explained her project for the nursing home, and a smile spread across Pastor Lake's features.

"What a great suggestion!"

Lexi sagged in her chair. "But it won't earn enough. There will still have to be other fund-raisers."

"It's a start. An excellent start, I think. Besides the line and the phone fees, we'd have to have training sessions for the volunteers who'd man the line. We aren't sure what our costs will be yet, but Will is researching that."

"I know Egg and Binky would like to help, too. And Todd, Peggy, Jennifer—"

"Do they make quilts, too?"

"Ha! It was like pulling teeth to get them to do one square! No, there's got to be something else. Let me think about it. That is, of course, if you'll let us help."

Chapter Six

"What do *you* want?" was Gina's ungracious greeting when Lexi knocked on the Williams' front door.

"Is Minda here?" Lexi ignored her rudeness.

"We're having a Hi-Five meeting," Gina said importantly.

"Great. That's perfect. Then I can talk to all of you at once." Lexi walked past Gina into the house. Minda, Tressa, Rita, and a couple girls Lexi didn't know by name were seated in the living room around a bowl of popcorn. The "meeting" looked very much like a gossip session.

Gina followed Lexi with a sour expression on her face. "Sorry about this, girls, but Lexi must be on a mission."

"Actually, I am. Can you spare a few minutes?"

Minda waved Lexi an invitation to join them on the floor. Lexi crossed her legs and dropped down between Rita and Tressa. There was a time when she never would have dreamed of being so bold around the Hi-Fives, but Lexi was learning that these girls didn't understand anything but bluntness. And as she'd come to suspect, they usually respected her more when she wasn't such a wimp.

She quickly explained the quilt she was making for the nursing home and her idea of having all her friends contribute a square.

"All your friends? And that includes us?" Gina asked.

Lexi smiled at her sweetly. "Why not? Everybody else is doing it. I wouldn't want you to feel left out."

"Who is everybody?" Tressa asked suspiciously. If these girls had a weak spot, it was not being in on the action.

Lexi listed the names. Even she had been surprised by how many students had heard about her quilt and volunteered to help. The quilt, which Lexi had planned to make for a twin bed, had grown to a queen size already.

"Wow," Tressa said. "I wouldn't have guessed that would be such a popular idea."

"It's for a good cause," Lexi commented.

"It wouldn't hurt us to do it, I suppose," Minda murmured thoughtfully. "Public relations and all that."

That was all it took. The other girls practically fell all over themselves volunteering to help. Lexi graciously accepted their offers and handed out the fabric and instructions. She even shared a cola with Rita before excusing herself to leave.

Minda walked her to the door. "It's pretty cool,

your idea about the quilt."

"You think so?" Lexi was surprised.

"I'm doing a report on volunteerism for history class," Minda continued. "Lots of stuff in this country might never have gotten done if it weren't for volunteers. Besides, I get ten extra-credit points if I volunteer for something."

Keeping all smart comments to herself, Lexi thanked Minda and left. If ten extra-credit points were what it took to get the Hi-Fives to work, fine. Then she grinned. The quilt plans were coming along nicely.

———————

"You've got to help me!"

Lexi recognized Binky's panicked voice at once.

"Can you come over? Now?"

Lexi glanced at the clock. It was six-thirty. "I suppose. We ate early tonight."

"Good." Binky's relief wafted over the phone line. "Someone's got to talk some sense into Egg. He's totally lost it. I've never seen him like this. He's so upset about Angela that he's beginning to scare me. Mom asked me if I'd call a friend to talk to him. Todd's on his way over, and I want you to come, too."

"I don't know if I can help. We're not counselors, Binky."

"I know, but can you try anyway? I don't know what else to do."

"I'll be right over."

Todd had already arrived. He and Egg were sitting at the kitchen table. Egg's mother was hovering in the doorway. Lexi saw the relief on her face when she entered. *Wow,* Lexi thought, *Egg must be pretty bad if his own parents don't know what to do for him.*

Egg looked up as she entered. He had been crying. His face was swollen and his lips were chapped. A pile of used tissues rested by his elbow.

"Egg, you're a mess!" Lexi blurted. Then she clapped a hand over her mouth. "I shouldn't have said that. I'm sorry. It's just that you look so . . ."

"Pitiful?" he finished for her. "That's what I am. Why shouldn't you say it? I'm a pitiful boyfriend, too. I should have helped Angela. Why didn't I listen when she said she was unhappy?"

"Because you never dreamed she'd go so far as to run away! Quit the pity party and pull yourself together." Todd was unrelenting. "You aren't doing her any good now, either, the way you're acting. How can being this upset help her?"

"What difference does it make?" Egg asked. "If I didn't help before, I certainly can't now." Then, as if a light had gone on in his brain, he added, "Can I?"

"Egg . . ." Binky warned. She'd seen that look on her brother's face before. "The police are handling it. Mrs. Hardy and Ted are doing what they can. Everything possible is being done."

"Everything? Are you sure? I'm not. *I* could be doing something, too. I *have* to do something!" He stood up and the chair he'd been sitting on fell backward onto the floor with a clatter. "Do you think they've questioned people at the mission yet?"

"I would think so," Lexi said. "After all, Angela and her mom lived there for a while. Mrs. Hardy had a job there, too."

"Well, I have to start somewhere. The mission is as good a place as any." Egg reached for his jacket. "Are you coming with me?"

"Just what is it you think you're going to do?" Binky asked.

"Angela knows people there. People who've been on the run before. I want to talk to them."

"The police have most likely done that," Todd reminded him gently.

"But they don't know Angela like I do. Maybe I can ask the right question and learn something they didn't."

"Egg, you don't think—"

But Lexi didn't let Binky finish. "Let him try," she said softly. "He has to try. I think we should go with him."

Binky, realizing that forcing Egg to sit at home and do nothing would be a disaster, gave in. "Then we'll *all* go."

———

"I think we're going too far to humor my brother," Binky hissed to Lexi as they walked toward the front door of the mission. "This isn't the best part of town to be hanging around at night."

"There are four of us," Lexi said, glad for Todd's strong arms and athletic body next to her.

Though the outside of the mission looked as though it could use some work, the inside was cheerful and inviting. A television was on somewhere in the distance, and she could hear people laughing. The light was still on in the director's office, and there were two figures inside. Lexi raised her hand to knock on the door.

"It's open. Come in," a voice called.

The foursome, feeling suddenly awkward, stepped into the large open area that made up the foyer. To their left a movable chalkboard stood slightly tilted, and to their right a bulletin board full of notices and tracts hung neatly on the wall. Someone had scrawled "God Lives!" on the chalkboard. Underneath it, in a different hand, was the word "Amen."

"Can I help you?" A man dressed in jeans and a white T-shirt walked up to them.

"We're looking for the mission director," Lexi said. They'd all met Will Adams while Angela and her mom were still living at the mission. "Is he here?"

"I'll get him." The man disappeared down a short hall. When he returned, Will was with him.

"Hello!" Mr. Adams looked surprised.

"Do you remember me, Mr. Adams?" Lexi began. "I'm Lexi Leighton, and these are my friends Todd, Egg, and Binky. I met you when—"

"Of course. I remember all of you. You're

Angela's friends. And please call me Will."

"Have you heard from her?" Egg blurted.

"No. I'm sorry. The police have already been here. They had hoped the same thing." Will gestured them into a cozy living room-like area where they all sat down.

"You don't have *any* idea about where she might have gone?" Egg's voice was pleading.

"None. Angela stopped by last week to say hello. She did seem distracted, but I had no inkling that she was so upset. Frankly, even if I *had* known, I wouldn't have been much help. I've met Ted. He's a wonderful man. He's volunteered here for holiday dinners, and he's been generous with donations, as well. I would have thought Angela would be delighted that her mother had such a fine friend."

"She's afraid," Lexi said softly. "Afraid of losing her mother and their relationship."

Will sighed. "But running away doesn't solve anything. I only wish our new center had been up and running."

"What center?" Binky asked.

"This seems very ironic, considering what has happened with Angela, but the mission has recently been considering opening a runaway center."

"Here? In Cedar River? Isn't that the kind of thing you find in big cities?" Todd asked.

"That's true, but a number of young people have found their way to our mission. Apparently, word is out that we are sympathetic and helpful. I've been working with one of the local churches. Pastor Lake has been an invaluable help." Will looked at his watch. "In fact, he should be here shortly to discuss our project."

"I never thought of helping runaways as a church project, but it should be," Binky mused.

"Makes sense to me," Todd agreed. He looked up as someone entered the area where they were sitting.

"Pastor Lake!" Lexi said. "We were just talking about you!"

"I take it you're looking for your friend Angela," he said gently as he sat down across from the group. "Have you found her yet?"

"We thought we might learn something here," Egg said. "But it's a dead end."

"Not really," Lexi corrected. "We're learning more about runaways."

"While I was in college," Pastor Lake said, "I volunteered at a center like the one we're trying to start here. It was a real eye-opener for me. Because I came from a happy home, I had no idea how many miserable, desperate kids were out there. We want to help as many runaways as we can with the new center."

"What will it be like?" Binky asked. She looked around the mission great room. "Like this?"

"There's really no set pattern. They are as different as the kids who come to them. Some are run by churches, others by a city, or even the kids themselves. Sometimes kids are only allowed to stay at the shelter a few days, while at others, a few make it their permanent home. The second is the kind of place I worked at."

"What was it like?" Egg wondered.

"It reminded me of a college dorm . . . kids living together, playing music, fighting, talking. Some go to school, others work."

"Sounds like one big party to me," Binky said with a snort. "Maybe we should all move out."

Pastor Lake smiled. "Oh, there are rules, all right. But for kids who've lived out of trash cans on the streets, it's pretty silly to come down too hard on them for being fifteen minutes late for curfew. The most important thing is to give them counseling, healthy role models, structure for their lives, and better ways to handle their problems. If we pushed too hard, they'd just run again anyway."

"And do their parents know where they are?"

"Oh yes. Often it's a big relief for parents to know that their child is safe and in competent hands. We try to prepare kids to go home again. Kids who stayed at our center had regular meals, counseling, a roof over their heads, and protection from all the trash out there that feeds on vulnerable children."

"But not every runaway finds a place like that, do they?" It was obvious that Egg was thinking about Angela.

"No," Will said. "Those are the long-term residential facilities. Actually, what we'd like to develop first is a crisis intervention center. It's a place that can give immediate help—a meal, a bed, a counselor, someone who cares. A runaway needs to get off the streets, to break the cycle. Social workers use a place like that to house someone the police has turned over to social services. Kids wait there until their parents come to pick them up. Sometimes, if a runaway doesn't feel ready to go home, the counselors can arrange a neutral place to meet."

Pastor Lake looked at Egg and understood what he was concerned about. "The police know about all these services and shelters, Egg. Any time they pick up a runaway, they know what to do."

"I still don't get it," Binky grumbled. "I don't see why anyone would want to run away. It sounds horrible!"

"Sometimes kids are running from something pretty dreadful, too," Will said. "Unstable or broken homes, alcohol abuse, conflict, drugs—things kids with happier lives can't even imagine."

"But Angela didn't have anything like that. She was just getting her life together!" Egg protested. "Her mom is nice. Ted seems like a good guy. Angela has a real home now. Why would she even think of leaving it?"

"I have to agree with Egg," Binky said. "We don't always have it so great at our house. Our parents don't have a lot of time *or* money, but it's sure a lot better there than on the street."

"We can't judge the situations of others. People don't know exactly what goes on inside a home unless they live there. Sometimes runaways come from the most unexpected homes—homes that *seem* to be happy," Will observed.

"But *why*?" Egg persisted.

Will looked thoughtful. "Issues not dealt with when they should have been. Kids who weren't asked to take responsibility for their actions. Parents who made excuses for them. A lack of limits. I counseled a boy who'd been in trouble a number of times. Each time it happened, his parents seemed to take the attitude "boys will be boys" and did little about the problem. Soon this young man realized that he didn't have any limits, and his parents lost all influence over him."

"If he was the boss, why would he even want to run away?" Todd asked. "Wouldn't he rather have stayed?"

"The more trouble he got into, the angrier his parents became. Feeling helpless, his parents began to argue with him and criticize his behavior. Before long, the relationship deteriorated to the point that they were fighting almost continually. What looked like a normal household on the outside was actually a miserable place for him to live."

"But Angela and her mother weren't having any trouble at all until Ted came along," Binky pointed out.

"Sometimes the impetus to run away is even less than what sent Angela off—being in trouble for breaking curfew or being told they can't go out with friends, for example."

"I don't know how she figured this could help," Egg muttered.

"Maybe she didn't think it would," Will said. "Sometimes running is a cry for help. It's my personal opinion that Angela wants to be found. What I think she's really saying is, 'Ask my opinion, Mom. Consult me before turning my life upside down.'"

Just then the young man who had opened the door to them came in carrying a tray filled with sodas, glasses, and a plate of chocolate cookies. He set it down on a nearby table.

"The police just called," he said to Will. "They're bringing someone by."

Will's eyebrow arched. "Oh?"

"A social worker will meet them here. It's a girl they picked up at the bus station. They said she looked lost and confused. I don't know if she's said much else, but they wanted her to come here because they thought it would be the least frightening place for an interview."

Will nodded, and the young man disappeared. He looked at Pastor Lake. "Another validation that we should be going ahead with the plans for a shelter."

"It wouldn't be Angela, would it?" Binky asked.

"That's doubtful. I can't imagine that she'd hang around the bus depot, but—"

Before Will could say more, the front door opened and Officer Bendle entered with a tall, slender girl of about seventeen. She had long, dusky blond hair, gray-green eyes, and lovely angular features. She looked more like a model than a runaway. There were shadows beneath her eyes and a sullen expression on her face.

Will jumped to his feet and ushered them into his office. Within moments, the social worker arrived to join them.

"Should we leave?" Todd wondered aloud after a long wait.

"No!" Egg was adamant. "I want to talk to her."

"Are you crazy?" Binky hissed.

"I'm going to ask her about Angela," Egg insisted.

"How would she know anything about that?" Binky scoffed. "Just because she's a runaway doesn't mean she knows Angela!"

"Who is Angela?"

They were startled to see the social worker standing behind them. Will, Officer Bendle, and the girl were nearby. The interview was obviously over.

Quickly, Will explained their concerns about Angela. "This is very difficult for them," he said, looking at Egg compassionately. "It's hard to accept that their friend could vanish so quickly."

"But I *might* know something!" the young girl spoke up. The adults stared at her, dumbfounded.

"I met a girl yesterday . . . at a rest stop and picnic area on the outskirts of town." She went on to describe the girl. Lexi couldn't have described Angela better. "She said she was going to hitchhike. She asked me what kind of luck I'd had doing it," the girl said timidly. Her voice was soft and tired.

"What did you tell her?" Pastor Lake asked gently.

Tears sprung into the girl's gray-green eyes. "I told her not to do it. I told her it was hard and scary. People don't pick up hitchhikers much anymore, and I'm not sure it's safe to trust some of those that do. I got scared a couple times. Once, a guy I was riding with turned off the road. I knew he was going to take me somewhere I didn't want to be, so I jumped out of the car when he slowed down to take a turn."

"You jumped out of a moving car?" Binky gasped.

The girl looked at her levelly. "It was better than what I suspected was coming."

"Did you tell Angela . . . I mean, this girl you met . . . about this?"

"Yes. We sat on a bench in the rest area for a long time. I guess I've been pretty bummed. Running away isn't like I thought it would be. I tried to tell her, but she wouldn't listen. She said she was really mad at her mother—something about a guy she was dating. I told her that I'd been mad when I left, too, but home was beginning to sound better and better."

The girl looked at the floor. "I suppose I'd already made up my mind to find someone to help me get home, but talking to her made me positive it was what I wanted. Crummy as it felt at home, it's *nothing* like being on the run."

"It was Angela!" Egg jumped up from the couch.

He grabbed Officer Bendle's hand. "Go get her!"

The young girl laughed bitterly. "Oh, she's long gone. She got a ride with a truck driver. I saw her go."

At that, Officer Bendle stepped forward with a series of rapid-fire questions about the truck, the driver, and the direction in which the truck had traveled. When she'd extracted all the information the girl had, she excused herself to use the telephone.

Throughout the questioning, Egg's expression alternated between joy and despair. He jumped to his feet when the police officer left the room. "Can you tell me what she said?" he pleaded. "Tell me everything."

The girl, whom the social worker called Sandra, chewed thoughtfully on her lower lip. "We just talked about why we'd left home. I told her about my mom, that after Dad died, she started staying home and wanting me to stay with her. It was as if she couldn't get along without me. It wasn't that I didn't love my mother or that she didn't love me, but she was smothering me.

"I couldn't be in any extracurricular activities because she needed me at home. She got upset when I went out on dates. My friends quit coming over because Mom wouldn't leave them alone. I think I could have taken it if it hadn't been for the way she treated Bennie."

"Bennie?"

"Ben Jayson, my boyfriend. Mom didn't think I

was old enough or mature enough to have a boyfriend. But Bennie and I were really more friends
than romantic. We got together and talked mostly.
Or I'd talk and he'd listen. After Mom said no about
Ben, we started meeting in secret. When Mom
found that out . . ." She drew a deep sigh. "That's
when I decided to run away."

"What about Bennie?"

Sandra's eyes clouded with tears. "He was supposed to meet me. He *said* he would!"

"But he didn't?"

"My mother told his parents. I'm sure she did,
or he would have been there for me. Just because
my mother's starving for attention doesn't mean
she should ruin my life, too!"

Tears dripped down Sandra's cheeks. "I don't
care that Ben didn't meet me. I had to get away."
She wiped her eyes and continued. "This girl—I
never got her name—said she knew how it felt. She
talked about how her mom was ignoring her for
some guy. She didn't have a plan or anything. Apparently she just decided to do it and left. I think
she was worried about money. Did your friend have
lots of money?"

Before anyone could respond, they heard
another knock on the front door.

"Busy place tonight," Will commented.

"That's probably your mother," the social worker
said to Sandra. "Would you like to go into Will's
office? I can bring her in there."

Sandra nodded and escaped to the privacy of the

office just before Will came through leading a nicely dressed woman who was wringing her hands with worry. She paused at the sight of the teenagers, her gaze scanning the faces for one that was familiar. "Sandra?" she whispered.

"She's in my office. It might be best if you meet first in private."

The woman nodded but didn't move. Lexi watched in dismay as the attractive woman crumpled before their eyes. The emotion that must have driven her this far now overtook her. Her face seemed to cave in, and she bit back a sob. Tears washed over her cheeks, trailing rivulets of mascara all the way to her chin.

It occurred to Lexi that the face before her embodied suffering in a way she'd never before experienced. How this woman must have been hurting . . . how frightened . . . how confused. *If kids knew what their running away really did to their parents, maybe they wouldn't leave in the first place*, she thought.

Gently, the social worker took the woman by the arm and led her into Will's office.

When they were alone again, Egg began to pace. "That settles it. We have to do something."

"Maybe we can." Lexi told them about the next quilt she'd offered to make to raise money for the hotline.

"That's good," Todd said. "But will it bring in much money?"

"I don't know. Maybe we could brainstorm and

come up with some other ideas."

"Like what?"

"Car washes? Bake sales?"

"Old ideas," Egg concluded bluntly. "They've been done too much."

"Then if you're so smart," Binky retorted, "you think of something we could all do that would make lots of money."

Egg frowned deeply as though he couldn't think without a great deal of facial effort. Then his forehead cleared. "I've got it! Singing telegrams!"

They all stared at him blankly.

"You know—having people hire us to deliver singing telegrams around town. We could do it for birthdays, anniversaries, any special occasion. Maybe the Emerald Tones could be in charge of it. Mrs. Waverly would go for the idea. I know she would."

"Actually, it's not a bad idea," Binky said.

"It's a great idea! Egg, you are brilliant!" Todd cried.

But Egg wasn't looking brilliant. He was looking depressed and scared. "We still have to do more," he said. Passion filled his voice. "We've got to find her." Egg's thin shoulders were squared and his jaw thrust forward with determination. "For Mrs. Hardy's sake, for our sakes, and especially for Angela's sake."

"Be realistic, Egg. What can we do?" Binky retorted.

"She can't have gone far," Egg persisted, ignoring his sister. "Yet."

"She's a day ahead of us," Todd pointed out.

Egg spun on him, his eyes flashing. "Well, I can't give up just like that! I have to do something." He choked on a sob. "Anything."

Then gathering control of his emotions once again, Egg suggested, "We could go to that rest stop and look for clues."

"At night?"

"After all this time?"

For a moment, Egg's face looked as though it would crumple just like Sandra's mother's had.

Todd, seeing the response, said quickly, "It can't hurt. It will give us something to do, and it's too late to talk to Mrs. Waverly about the singing telegrams tonight."

"Maybe you're right," Lexi said with a sigh. "Doing anything will feel better than doing nothing."

Together, they started for the park to search for what they already knew they would not find.

Chapter Seven

The picnic area was eerily quiet. Pinkish sodium lights spotted the pathways that the four followed through the grass. A dog yapped somewhere in the distance. Egg wandered forlornly, leading the other three in a disjointed pattern from one end of the rest stop to the other. Finally he dropped onto a bench and put his head in his hands.

"You were right. It's useless. I just thought if I could come here I'd know what Angela was thinking, and I'd suddenly know where she might have gone. Dumb, huh?"

"You had to try, Egg," Lexi said gently. She rubbed his shoulder and felt utterly helpless.

"Every hour she's gone it gets more scary."

"She hasn't been gone three days yet, Egg. Maybe she hasn't gotten very far."

"How can someone just disappear from your life?" he asked. "Angela knew how much we all cared for her. How could she do this to us?" Then tears began to stream down his cheeks. "How could she do it to herself? Something terrible could happen to her. She's trusting total strangers more than she'll trust the people who know and love her. Why?"

It didn't make sense, Lexi thought. Nothing about this entire situation did. How could someone just vanish?

They came in groups of twos and threes to Lexi's house, carrying their completed quilt blocks. Lexi's father greeted everyone at the door before escaping upstairs with his newspaper.

Peggy and Jennifer arrived first, followed by Todd and Tim, Anna Marie, and some of their friends from the *Cedar River Review* and the Emerald Tones. Binky and Egg arrived just before Minda Hannaford and Tressa and Gina Williams.

"What are they doing here?" Binky hissed to Lexi, jerking her head to indicate the group coming up the walk.

"They decorated quilt blocks for me, too. They're going to help us put it together."

"How did you get them to do that? I didn't think those girls ever did anything for anyone except themselves."

"Not unless it means they might miss out on a party," Lexi said with a chuckle. "When I told them that we'd put it together as a group and share some pizzas and sodas while we did it, they decided they *might* be able to spare a little time and effort."

"They're as bad as Egg. He'll go anywhere for

free food." Binky disappeared inside the house, leaving Lexi to greet her other guests.

"Hi. I'm glad you could come," she said to the three girls.

"You are?" Gina blurted. "I mean . . ."

"Never mind," Lexi said with a smile. "May I see your quilt blocks?"

They looked at one another hesitantly.

"We've never done anything like this before," Tressa began.

"I'm no Susie Homemaker," Minda warned. Slowly she handed Lexi their quilt blocks.

Lexi held them in her hands and stared. Finally she spoke. "These are beautiful!"

"They are?" Minda asked. "Really?"

"Absolutely. How clever."

The girls had taken their pieces of fabric to the little T-shirt shop at the mall, had their photos taken, and had their likenesses transferred to the quilt blocks. Minda's, Gina's, and Tressa's faces smiled out from the fabric to Lexi. Minda had even used makeup to give herself some color—blush, eyeshadow, and lipstick.

"We figured this would be the only quilt any of us might ever work on," Gina admitted sheepishly, "so we thought we'd better let people know who we are."

"I like it," Lexi said with sincerity. "This makes it totally different from any other quilt in existence. I might have to make a family quilt for Mom like this sometime."

"You mean *we* gave *you* an idea?" Tressa asked, surprised.

"Of course. I love it. Come inside and say hello to the others."

Everyone was trying their hardest to be festive, Lexi knew, but the mood in her living room was not very cheery. Even Minda and company were subdued. Angela's absence was weighing heavily on their minds. Benjamin, Wiggles, and the new kitten were the only happy-go-lucky ones in the room.

Ben had devised a bed for Lucky at the top of a carpet-covered scratching post. The kitten sat there like a miniature lion, bathing himself, ignoring Wiggles' whimpering and yipping beneath him.

"Ben, put Wiggles outside. He's making too much noise," Lexi finally ordered. "Then come in and show everyone what you made."

Ben grabbed Wiggles by the collar and scooted him out of the room. That was Lucky's signal to jump down from his perch and attack a long string dangling from the corner of Binky's quilt square.

When Ben returned, he was carrying his own square. He'd drawn a picture of Wiggles on the block with fabric paints. It was bright and childish and sweet.

Lexi gave everyone a work assignment. Some were in charge of food, others, laying out the squares in an attractive pattern, and still others, pinning the blocks together while she manned the sewing machine. Todd and Egg were in charge of the ironing board.

The doorbell rang in the middle of the chaos, and Matt Windsor sauntered into the room.

"Hurry up," Minda ordered. "We need your block." She scooped it out of his hands. She glanced at it once, then, pausing, she looked at it again, more thoroughly this time. "Matt, this is great!" she exclaimed.

Everyone stopped to study what Minda was holding. It *was* beautiful. Matt had made a detailed sketch of his motorcycle.

"I drew it, but my stepmom embroidered it," he said self-consciously.

"Come see the quilt. I'm still stitching it together." Lexi led him toward the dining room table where the quilt was spread out in colorful array. She took Matt's block and fitted it into one of two open spots. "Perfect."

The quilt did look wonderful. That was why everyone was surprised when Binky started to cry.

"Bink? What's wrong?" Lexi asked.

"Look." She pointed at the colorful patches. "Don't you see? We're missing a square. *Angela's* square. As long as that's not here, as long as *she's* not here, we can't be done. The quilt isn't complete . . . we aren't complete . . . without her."

After a long silence, Minda finally said, "I wonder where she is right now. Do you think she's hungry or anything? Did she take many clothes with her?"

Egg rolled his eyes and groaned loudly at Minda's last question.

"Well, it's a valid question," Minda said, defending herself. "How much could she carry? Wouldn't she want to be clean?"

"You couldn't run away, Minda, you'd need a bus to carry your stuff," Binky groused.

"Minda's right," Lexi said. "I never thought about what Angela might take with her."

"A toothbrush and toothpaste," someone suggested.

"Clean underwear and socks."

"A comb and brush."

"Money."

"But Angela didn't have much money," Egg said weakly.

"Then how would she eat? Where would she get food?"

That question seemed to overwhelm them all. Where *would* Angela eat? And sleep? And bathe? They'd brought up questions that had no answers. Everyone was quiet as they began to realize all of the things they'd always taken for granted. They'd never considered this before. Had Angela? Or had she run first and thought about it later?

The somber mood still hung over Lexi later when the party broke up. Matt had hung back until only Egg, Binky, Lexi, and Todd remained.

"So Angela hasn't tried to get in touch with anyone?" Matt asked.

"We've been talking to Mrs. Hardy every few hours," Lexi said. "I almost hate to call her anymore. She sounds so sad when she hears my voice on the phone instead of Angela's."

"My mom said she'd call immediately if Angela tried to call our place," Binky said. "We thought she might try to call Egg or Lexi but . . ."

Matt frowned and cleared his throat. "Nothing?"

"I wish I could do something," Egg said. "Anything!"

"I might know someone you could talk to," Matt said quietly.

They stared at him in disbelief.

"You know something?" Egg bolted out of his chair. "And you haven't said anything?"

"Settle down, Eggo. I don't know anything. All I'm saying is that I ran across someone who knows other kids in similar situations as Angela."

Lexi studied Matt intently. Every time she thought she was really getting to know him, he surprised her.

"Who? *Who?*" Egg grabbed Matt by the front of the shirt.

"Chill, McNaughton!" Matt shook him away and glared at him. He straightened his clothing. "Besides, I already asked him specifically about Angela. He doesn't know anything about her. It's just that he knows a lot about runaways, that's all." Matt looked sullen, as if he was sorry he'd said anything.

"I'm sorry," Egg said. "I just lost it for a minute. We'd appreciate any ideas or help we could get. Wouldn't we?" He gave Todd and Lexi a pleading glance.

"Why don't I introduce you to my friend?" Matt said grudgingly. "But you have to promise not to bug this guy. He's got enough problems already."

———————

The next afternoon, Todd, Lexi, Egg, and Binky met Matt at Mike's garage.

Todd's brother, Mike, looked up from the paper work he was doing in his office when they entered. "How's it going?"

"It's been better," Todd said.

"No word on Angela yet?"

Matt's entrance saved them from giving an answer. They all piled into Todd's car while Matt gave directions. Within minutes they pulled up in front of a condemned house near the railroad tracks not far from the mission. The house had broken shutters and a dismal gray cast that told them the structure had once been white. Missing panes of glass made the windows look like staring eyes. Splintered steps ran up to a sagging porch.

"Why are we at a deserted house?" Binky asked. "There's nobody within three blocks of this place."

Matt ignored her. Instead, he put two fingers to his lips and gave a piercing whistle. Then he called, "Mouse? Are you here?"

Binky squeaked. "Mice? No way. I'm getting out of here!"

Matt grabbed her by the arm. "Not mice, *Mouse*. It's a name. Now, be quiet."

A boy appeared then, seemingly out of nowhere.

He was thin and badly dressed, and his expression was that of extreme suspicion.

"What are you doing here?" Mouse said sharply to Matt. "And why did you bring them? You shouldn't have—"

"Have you seen or heard anything about the girl I asked you about?" Matt said, ignoring Mouse's anger.

"Nothing. But I told you—"

"I know, I know. No one but me was supposed to know about this place, and I promised on our friendship that I wouldn't tell anyone about it. But these guys are going crazy with worry. I thought maybe if they saw . . ."

Mouse gave an aggravated sigh. "Come on, then, you're making too much noise." And he turned and walked toward the rickety house.

"What is this place?" Lexi whispered.

"A hideout," Matt said shortly. "Come on."

A door on the far side of the house was open, and they followed Mouse inside. Much to Lexi's and the others' surprise, the inside of the house actually looked lived in.

There was a collection of shabby furniture around the room and even some chipped, mismatched dishes on the scarred old table in the center of the room. A gaunt-looking boy glanced up from the floor where he was sitting. His eyes were hollow and expressionless.

"Matt, I think you'd better explain," Todd said. "Now."

"Mouse and I knew each other a long time ago."
Matt no doubt referred to his much wilder days—a
time he usually disliked discussing. "I ran into him
one day a couple months ago, and we got reac-
quainted. He wasn't living with his stepfather anymore, and I wanted to know where he'd gone. That's
when he showed me this place. It's an underground
refuge home for runaways. Kids on the road just
hear about it and come."

Binky, Egg, Todd, and Lexi stared at Matt,
dumbfounded. "Here? In Cedar River?" Binky
squealed.

Mouse looked at Binky pityingly, as if she were
too innocent and naive to be for real. "It's close to
the mission so it's easy to get food. Besides, the
word is out that the people over there want to help
runaways."

"So why don't you just go there?" Egg asked.

"We might if we decide we can trust that Will
Adams. Until then it's not so bad here."

Not so bad? Lexi thought. *It's dreadful here.*

Two girls huddled on the couch. Mouse intro-
duced them as Sunny and Leah.

"You're staying here, too?" Binky was horrified.

"Only a couple days," Sunny said. "Leah and I
want to go to California. You know, warm weather,
movie stars. We think we can get work out there
and maybe be discovered. Wouldn't it be great to be
in the movies or on TV?"

She looked very pale, Lexi noticed. Sickly.

"But what about your families?" Binky blurted.

The expressions on the girls' faces hardened.

"What about them?" Leah said. "They're the reason we left home. Why would we want to go back?"

Binky looked so confused and dismayed that Leah continued. "My parents have been fighting since I was a little kid. I never got used to it, but when they started smacking *me* around, I decided it was time to get out. I'd run away before but didn't get very far.

"My folks always apologize the next day when they're sober, but it never lasts. Lately, I've been scared of my dad when he's drinking. I know he'd never mean to hurt me, but he's like a stranger when he's drunk."

Sunny rubbed Leah's arm comfortingly as she spoke. It was apparent that the two girls were their own support system.

Then Leah continued. "But Sunny had it even worse than me. At least I didn't have a weird relative trying to touch me when my parents weren't around!"

"Leah, shhh!" Sunny looked frightened and ashamed.

"It wasn't your fault nobody believed you! You had no choice but to leave!"

Sunny started to cry.

Leah continued her story. "Sunny was afraid that if she didn't get away, her cousin might do more than trap her alone and run his hands all over her."

"There are phone numbers you can call to report that kind of thing!" Lexi spoke up. "We learned about that in school. You didn't need to run away to get help."

"I'd like to go home," Sunny said sadly. "But not if my cousin is there. It's weird, but I thought running away would help—that it would be different . . . easier. I didn't plan very well. I just took off. No clothes, no money. I've never been so tired or hungry before in my life." Sunny looked at Leah. "Or lonesome. Until I found Leah, that is." Tears sprung to Sunny's eyes. "And I've discovered that there are weird guys like my cousin everywhere. I can't trust anyone."

She coughed then, a harsh, wracking cough that came from deep within her. She wiped her running nose on the sleeve of her sweat shirt.

Impulsively, Lexi reached out and put her hand on Sunny's forehead. Lexi felt as though she'd touched her fingers to a griddle.

"You're burning up!" she exclaimed.

Mouse looked concerned. "You didn't say you were sick!"

"Leave her alone," Leah retorted. "Sunny? Are you going to be all right?"

"You've got to get her some help," Lexi said. "She's very sick. Let's go get Will Adams and Pastor Lake. They can help you."

"No!" three voices chimed in unison.

"You can trust them," Matt assured the trio.

"You don't know anything," Mouse growled. "We

thought we could trust adults, and look what happened to us."

Sunny shivered and had a coughing fit that left her curled up in a ball.

Lexi grew uncharacteristically angry. "Not everyone is bad, you know! There are people who *can* be trusted. Are you going to let her get sicker and sicker because you won't give anyone a chance to help you?" She knelt by Sunny and brushed a strand of hair from her eyes. "Will and Pastor Lake won't fail you. I promise."

"No way!" Mouse bellowed. "It will wreck what we've got here. It will ruin everything."

"Chill out, Mouse," Matt ordered. "She's *sick*."

The argument might have continued if Sunny had not suddenly given a little groan and fainted.

Leah screamed. Mouse turned pale.

Todd grabbed Lexi by the hand. "Come on. Lexi and I will go get help. The rest of you stay here."

Over Mouse's weak protests, Todd and Lexi hurried outside.

———

They were in luck. Pastor Lake was sitting in Will's office when they arrived, out of breath and flushed.

"Taking up jogging?" Will asked. "Sounds like you need it. You're winded."

"Will, you've got to help us!" Breathing heavily but still able to talk, Todd told them about their quest for Angela and how they'd come upon the kids living in the abandoned house. "And one of them is sick. Sunny—I don't know her last name—is sick. The boy who seems to be in charge over there didn't want us to come, but we insisted. We told them that you and Pastor Lake would help them. We promised you wouldn't disappoint them."

Will picked up the phone and called his secretary. "We'll have some extras staying here tonight. Please make sure there are fresh beds, towels, and food. And call a doctor to come over here, will you? I think we'll need a house call."

"Show us where to go," Pastor Lake insisted as both men stood.

———

When they reached the house, Egg was standing guard at the door. "Matt told me to stay here so nobody left." Poor Egg was white as a sheet.

"At ease, Egg. We'll take over now," Will reassured him.

Shortly after the men entered the house, Binky and Matt emerged.

"Those guys are pretty cool," Matt said with admiration. "They even got Mouse to settle down."

"What do we do now?" Egg croaked.

"Go home, I guess. There's nothing to do here."

"But I'll go nuts if I have to go home!" Egg looked panicked.

Will, who'd returned to thank them for doing the right thing, heard Egg's comment.

"Why don't you kids use my office?" he suggested. "Make lists of what you have to do to get the singing telegram thing off the ground. Then, if you aren't too tired, look at the calendar. We're already talking to the phone company about the installation of the hotline. Our next step is a campaign to train volunteers to work on it. Since there is a staff in the mission around the clock, we'll train them first, but we also want people from the community to be involved." He looked at the gaggle of weary, worried kids. "I'd guess that there are some potential volunteers right here."

Eager to keep busy and glad for an assignment, they made their way to Will's office at the mission. The silent agreement was that they'd wait there until they'd made all the plans Will had requested. They wanted to hear from Will himself that Sunny would be all right.

Chapter Eight

"Lexi, can I stay with you tonight?" Binky's voice was small. What they'd seen at the old house had shaken them all to the core. "I'd like to be with a friend tonight."

"Sure." Lexi was glad. She didn't feel much like being alone, either. "You can borrow some pajamas."

"Great. I'll go home in the morning and get ready for church. Tell Mom, won't you, Egg?"

Todd dropped them off at Lexi's driveway.

Mrs. Leighton was sitting in the kitchen, reading a magazine and drinking a cup of hot chocolate. "Hi, girls. Water is hot. Want some cocoa?"

"Sounds great, Mom. Are there any marshmallows?"

When the girls were settled at the table, Mrs. Leighton studied them over the rim of her mug. "Want to talk about it?"

"About what?" Lexi asked innocently.

"Whatever is bothering you, of course. Neither

of you are very good at hiding your emotions. Something's happened."

"Are *all* mothers mind readers?" Binky grumbled.

"It's a gift." Mrs. Leighton smiled at Binky. "Wait till you have kids, then you'll understand."

"I don't think I'll have any," Binky murmured. "It's too hard." Then she told Mrs. Leighton about the runaways they'd visited, the house, and Sunny.

Mrs. Leighton listened with a troubled expression on her features. "Oh my," she said when Binky was done.

"I keep asking myself what I—we—should have done to help Angela," Binky said sadly. "I kept seeing her face when I looked at Sunny and Leah. Those girls must have had friends, too—ones that didn't do anything to stop them from leaving. Can you tell me, Mrs. Leighton, what a person should do if her friend wants to run away?"

Mrs. Leighton rolled her mug between her palms and thought about Binky's question. "Don't be too hard on yourself, Binky. I know you did what you could. You listened when Angela was angry and didn't criticize, right?"

"Yes, but—"

"And you told Angela that she should give things time to get better?"

"We all did that. But what would *you* have done?" Binky's brow furrowed.

"If she told me she'd thought of running away, I'd probably try to talk her out of it. If I couldn't, I'd tell her every place I could think of that might be able to help her—churches, family crisis centers, shelters . . ."

"If I'd known what she was thinking, I would have told her mother or Will Adams," Binky said.

"But you couldn't read her mind," Mrs. Leighton said firmly. "So you can't be so critical of yourself."

"I keep thinking about Angela's mother," Lexi said. "She must be losing her mind. She tries to be brave when we talk to her, but I can hear the fear in her voice. Egg stops in to see her, and he says she looks terrible. How do you think it will be if—when—Angela comes home?"

"They'll have to work out a climate of respect and love for each other. Communication will be a key. All the things that should always be going on in a home."

As she spoke she looked at the new pillow-filled basket on the floor near the stove. Ben had finally managed to convince his parents he needed another pet. This time it was a stray kitten that had been brought to Dr. Leighton's office while Ben was there. "This is one lucky cat," Dr. Leighton had muttered. And the name stuck.

They talked until Binky's head began to bob and wobble and she couldn't keep her eyelids open any longer. Then, gathering Lucky out of his little basket, they went to Lexi's room. The kitten curled between them on the bed, his purring reminding Lexi of a gentle little snore.

Lucky was kneading the bedspread and Binky's

leg with his tiny, needlelike claws as she and Lexi talked softly. The girls were just drifting off to sleep when the telephone rang.

Lexi sat bolt upright and dove for the phone on the bedside stand. "Hello?"

"Lexi?" The voice was hoarse but familiar.

"Angela?"

Binky sprung up like a jack-in-the-box!

"Where are you?" Lexi demanded.

"I can't tell you," Angela replied.

"Of course you can tell me! We've been worried sick about you!" Lexi lowered her voice. "Angela, come home. Don't do this to us. Don't do it to *you*. I know things will work out. Will Adams and Pastor Lake will help you."

Angela started crying. "I don't know what to do, Lexi. How did I get myself into this mess? I'm so scared. . . ."

"Angela, listen to me. Your mother is frantic. She is so worried about you. I know she'll try to work out everything between you. You don't have to be afraid. No one is angry, only worried. Tell me where you are, and I'll have Egg drive out to get you. . . ."

"How is Egg? I miss him. I've been so lonely. Tell him not to worry, okay?" The roar of a motor drowned out Angela's voice for a moment.

"He can't help worrying! None of us can. We love you, Angela, and we've all been praying that you're all right and that you'll come home. Just tell me where you are. . . ." The sound of more revving motors filled the phone line.

"I can't. I'm still so confused. I have to think."

"You can do that with us. Stay at my house or Binky's. . . ."

"I've got to go. Tell Egg hi." The line went dead.

Lexi dropped the receiver and raced into her parents' room. "Angela just called! She wouldn't say where she was, but I could hear big noises in the background—trucks or something."

Dr. Leighton immediately picked up the phone and dialed the police. Within fifteen minutes, Officers Truman and Bendle were at the door asking for Lexi.

"She didn't say where she was, but there was a lot of noise in the background—motors maybe."

"Like semi trucks?" Officer Bendle asked, her pen scribbling furiously to record Lexi's every word.

"Could have been." Lexi thought about it. "Yes, I think so."

"A truck stop," Truman said. "It's a place to start. Do you think she was calling long distance?"

"I doubt it. I don't think she has much money with her."

"Then that certainly limits the number of gas stations and truck stops." Bendle nodded. "I'll get on it immediately."

After they left and Binky and Lexi had returned to the bedroom, the girls sat down side by side on the bed. There was nothing left to do but hope—and pray.

In the morning, Binky rolled over and nearly squashed Lucky, who was still asleep on the bed. "I can't go home this morning."

"Why not?" Lexi stretched and yawned in the same manner as the kitten.

"I don't want to face Egg yet. I'll have to tell him Angela called and that you couldn't get her to give you her location. He'll go ballistic."

"Maybe you're right. You can wear something of mine if we can find something small enough. But you *will* have to tell Egg sometime, you know."

"Just not yet, Lexi. Please?"

"After Sunday school, then. He'll be even more upset if you wait too long."

"I wish we didn't have to go to Sunday school today." Binky wrinkled her nose. "I'll never be able to pay attention."

But Binky was wrong.

When they got to the education rooms at the church, Todd met them. "We're meeting in the main room today. There's a special speaker."

"Really? That's a switch," Lexi replied.

They walked into the large room as students were setting up chairs and generally creating a great deal of noise. Pastor Lake directed the operation and finally marshaled them into the chairs. Lexi, Binky, and Todd slipped into the seats Egg was saving for them but didn't have a chance to speak before Pastor Lake went to the microphone.

After the opening prayer, Lexi glanced around the room and noticed a woman from the congregation seated at the back of the room. Although she couldn't remember her name, Lexi recognized her. She led the church choir sometimes. Lexi had also seen her working with some of the people who came to church on crutches or with canes or wheelchairs. It had always seemed to Lexi that the woman had infinite patience with others.

"Today we have a special need," Pastor Lake began. "As most of you know, Angela Hardy has run away. I know there are questions and concerns about Angela and about the drastic measure she has taken. I'd like to open this hour to discussion. It's important that we emphasize there are much better ways of dealing with problems at home than by running away.

"Sometimes things happen in a family that are unpleasant or even hurtful, but no matter how difficult the problem or how frightening the situation, running away can't solve it. There are people to talk to and places to go right here in your own hometown, and I think we should discuss the ramifications of running away and the other choices we have.

"I've asked a member of our congregation to come and speak to you today, someone who knows firsthand what it's like to be a teenage runaway."

Lexi sat straight up in her chair. Egg and Binky

leaned forward, looking around. Who could this be? Then the woman at the back of the room stood up.

"This is Charla Winger. Maybe some of you know her. Mrs. Winger has been very active with our church choir. Mrs. Winger, would you like to come up?"

The assembly of students stared at her as if she'd landed from another planet, and a low buzz of whispering filled the room.

"Her?" Binky gasped.

"She doesn't *look* like a runaway," Egg observed.

Binky jabbed him in the stomach with her elbow. "People don't have to look like runaways to be them, you know!"

"And what exactly does a runaway look like?" Todd asked, amused.

"Shhh. She's going to talk."

Mrs. Winger stood in front of them, her makeup applied flawlessly, her hair and clothes neat and attractive—a regular woman who looked a lot like their mothers!

"Surprised?" was the first word out of the woman's mouth.

Kids nodded.

"I thought you might be. It's hard to imagine a woman like your mom running away from home, isn't it? But that was a long time ago, and at the time, I thought I *had* to get away. I'd just had my sixteenth birthday and was sure that my life was going nowhere. I saw myself as an adventurer, a free spirit. And I felt trapped, like a butterfly in a mayonnaise jar. So I left."

"You weren't mad at your folks or anything?" someone asked.

"I was angry with everyone. They all seemed boring and materialistic to me."

"You were a hippie!" Egg blurted.

Mrs. Winger smiled. "Sort of. It sounds silly now, but at the time, I thought it was the bravest, smartest thing I could do. I was going to find my *own* life and show my parents that they really didn't know what was best for me."

"And did you?" Pastor Lake asked.

Mrs. Winger laughed. "What I discovered was it wasn't easy to live without all those things my parents had been providing, like food, shelter, and money. At first I thought it was kind of glamorous, striking out on my own. I was a rebel. Of course, it's hard to feel glamorous when you haven't washed your hair for a week."

"How long did you stay away?" Todd asked.

"I was gone several weeks. Then I got sick." Mrs. Winger's eyes clouded. "I'd made it to Chicago and was living in an abandoned warehouse with several other teenagers. I suppose if I'd been at home, I'd have told my mother when I started to feel bad and she would have taken me to the doctor. But I didn't think I needed my mother, and I certainly didn't have money for health care, so I let it go. It wasn't until I passed out that anyone else even realized that I was ill."

"What was wrong?" a girl in the front row asked.

"Kidney problems. But of course, no one knew that. They just knew they didn't want me around like that, so they dragged me outside and laid me on a park bench where a policeman found me. I woke up in a hospital."

Everyone looked horrified. "Your *friends* did that?"

"They weren't the good friends I'd thought they were, and they were all running, too. That was about the time I realized parents were a really good thing to have."

Lexi stared at the woman, aghast. *Could all of this really have happened to her?*

"My parents had been looking for me all this time, of course," Mrs. Winger continued. "And it didn't take long for them to reach the hospital."

"Were you glad?"

"I cried like a baby. I was very ill, and it was a long time before I was strong enough to go home. Mom and Dad took care of me." Her eyes filled with tears. "They forgave me for causing them so much pain and were so happy to take me back into their home."

"So everything turned out all right?" Egg asked hopefully.

Mrs. Winger looked sad. "I missed out on a lot of happy times. What's more, I had kidney damage from not taking care of myself. I still have to deal with that today."

"Would you do it again?" Pastor Lake asked.

"Not in a million years. And that's really what I

came here to talk to you about. Don't even consider running away as a solution to your problems. There isn't anything that can't be made better by facing the issue. But don't try to do it alone. There are pastors, teachers, relatives, friends, social agencies—lots of people—to ask for help. And they are much more accessible while you're still in school. On the road, you become more worried about where to find a bathroom or where to sleep than about solving that problem you had."

They were all quiet as they filed out of the Sunday school room to go to church. Mrs. Winger had made running away feel very real—and very foolish.

Later, during the sermon, Lexi felt tears stinging her eyes as Pastor Lake talked about the lost sheep and the Shepherd who valued each so much. It seemed like everything she heard lately related to Angela in some way or another.

On the way out of the church, Binky whispered to Lexi, "I think I'd better tell him now."

Egg and Todd were waiting for them on the sidewalk. Binky swallowed hard before grabbing her brother by the arm. "Don't talk."

"Huh? What's going on?"

"I said don't talk! I have something to tell you."

Egg paled. "It's about Angela, isn't it?"

"She called Lexi last night."

Egg spun to Lexi. "What did she say?"

"Very little. She wouldn't tell me where she was. I told her to come home, but she said she wasn't ready. I think she wants to. She's lonely and scared but stubborn."

"I want you to repeat *every word* she said. Every word, Lexi."

When Egg was finally satisfied that there was no more Lexi could tell him, his shoulders sagged and his whole demeanor drooped. "So we don't know any more than we did before."

"Yes, we do. We know that she's alive. We suspect that she called from a truck stop not too far away. And the police are out looking for her. That's a lot more than we knew yesterday."

"Well, it's not enough," Egg said angrily before walking away.

Chapter Nine

"Who's hungry for pancakes?" Mrs. Leighton asked as they pulled into the driveway.

Lexi hoped her mother wouldn't notice her lack of enthusiasm for food. Ever since she'd talked to Angela, her stomach had been in knots. She felt as if she'd failed—not managing to convince her friend that she should come home.

Lexi walked into the kitchen, dragging her hand across the counter. It was just a coincidence that she noticed the light flashing on the answering machine. She punched the replay button and listened absentmindedly for the message.

"Lexi? It's Angela. I know you're probably at church, but I just wanted you to know that I'm home." Her exhausted voice quavered. "I got so homesick after I talked to you last night, and then some police officers stopped to ask me some questions. I guess I didn't do a very good job of answering because the next thing I knew, they were whipping out a photograph of me and telling me to get in the car. Anyway, I'm back. I'm going to sleep now.

I think I could sleep for days."

Lexi replayed the message for her mom and dad, then called both Todd and the McNaughtons to give them the news. Finally feeling really hungry for the first time since Angela left, she happily offered to help her mother with lunch.

———————

At five o'clock that afternoon, Lexi decided that if she didn't do something she was going to burst. "I'm going to Angela's!" she announced.

"Are you sure that's a good idea?" Mrs. Leighton asked. "After all, she did say she was exhausted. You shouldn't disturb her."

"Then her mom can tell me to go away. I just have to go," Lexi said. She grabbed her jacket and headed out the door.

When she arrived at the Hardy's, Ted answered the door. He smiled when he saw it was Lexi. "Welcome. We were just talking about you. Come in."

Angela was sitting at the kitchen table, wrapped in a big fuzzy blanket. She had dark blotches beneath her eyes. Her skin had broken out in angry pimples.

"Lexi?" Angela looked up, and her weary expression brightened.

Without speaking, Lexi ran to the table and gathered Angela into her arms. "I was afraid I'd never see you again."

"Looks like you can't get rid of me that easily." Angela choked on the words.

"Do you girls want some privacy?" Mrs. Hardy asked. Her face was alight with relief and happiness.

"That's okay," Angela said. "You and Ted are welcome to stay . . . in fact, I want you to."

Lexi was surprised by Angela's change in attitude but said nothing. If Angela was getting along better with Ted and her mother, that was an answer to prayer.

Angela turned to face Lexi. "Even though I told you on the phone I wasn't ready to come back home, I was trying my hardest to get here. I hated running. I was scared and lonely." She looked at her mother. "But I did have a lot of time to think."

"So you were all alone this whole time?" Lexi asked.

"Not exactly. I did meet a couple other runaways. I met a girl at a rest stop. She kept hanging around after all the cars had left, and I realized she was alone, too. We stayed together for a while after that. It was nice to have company."

"Why had she left home?"

"She was pregnant, and her dad kicked her out of the house. She was trying to get to her grandmother's place. She thought her grandmother would take her in, at least till the baby was born."

"How sad!" Lexi replied.

"Everything is sad about runaways, as far as I can tell," Angela agreed. "I thought it was an answer to my problems, but I was wrong." Her eyes filled with tears. "I don't know if I can ever say I'm sorry enough times to make up for what I did."

Mrs. Hardy bent to put her arms around her daughter. "You're here now. That's enough."

"I wasn't fair to you, Mom, or Ted. I had plenty of time to realize that. Being lonely is lousy. I hated it." She paused, glancing again at Lexi. "Then I realized that maybe Mom had been lonely for a long time. She never complained, but since I found friends in Cedar River, I haven't been around much. I realized that I'd been wrong to be mad at her. I should have been *happy* she found someone." Angela glanced across the table at Ted. "That's why I was glad to hear their news."

"News?" Lexi looked curiously at the adults.

"Ted and I are planning to get married." Angela's mother practically glowed as she spoke. "And Angela is going to be my maid of honor. Ted and I had decided that we wouldn't go through with it if Angela didn't approve. If we ever got her back, we didn't want her to leave again. But if she could find it in her heart to accept him . . ."

"Ted wants to be a real father to me, Lexi. He said so. I've never had a father."

"Until now," Ted said. His expression was gentle as he looked at Angela. "I love your mother, and believe it or not, even after all the trouble you've caused, I love you, too. I've wanted a family for a long time. Nothing would make me happier than getting one ready-made." His expression grew stern. "But we *never* want another scare like the one we just had . . . please?"

"It's going to be hard to share my mom, but it's a lot better than never seeing her at all," Angela admitted somberly. Then she smiled. "But being a family—with a dad . . . I never thought I'd have that."

"We won't do anything too rash, Angela," her mother assured her. "Our decisions will be mutual ones. And no marriage until you are totally comfortable with the idea."

"They say I have to go to counseling," Angela murmured, looking at Lexi again.

"All of us will go," Ted corrected her. "The problems aren't Angela's alone. We'll share the tough times as well as the happy ones."

Lexi was impressed. She hardly knew Ted, but it was obvious the love he felt for Angela and her mom was real. She could see it in his expression.

Mrs. Hardy stood up and beckoned Ted to follow her. "Let's go into the living room. I think Lexi and Angela would like to visit alone now."

After they'd left the kitchen, Lexi turned her full attention to Angela. "I'm so glad you're back. You scared us, you know."

Angela's face crumpled and tears flooded her eyes. "I don't know how I'm going to face everyone. I'm so ashamed of what I've done. I can't stand the thought of going back to school with everyone knowing how stupid I've been."

"Well, you know that running away from a problem doesn't help. Maybe facing it head on will work the best. Go back with your head held high. *Say* you made a mistake and that it was dumb. Say it before Minda or anyone else has a chance to say it for you. Besides, everyone will be so happy to see you and to know that you're okay, that what's passed will stay in the past."

"Do you really think so?" Angela asked, wiping a tear away with the back of her hand.

"Absolutely," Lexi reassured her. "And if anyone does say something unpleasant to you, I'm sure Egg will straighten them out. He'll no doubt attach himself to you like a leech and never let go."

Angela smiled wanly. "Poor Egg. I can hardly wait to see him, but I told him to wait until tonight to come over. I thought I'd be able to sleep this afternoon, but my mind is still racing and I couldn't rest."

"Maybe I'd better go so you can try again."

"No, please don't. I don't like being alone with my thoughts."

"Not everything about this is bad, you know."

Angela looked surprised. "No? Name one thing."

"The mission is going to open its door to runaways. Will Adams is already looking for another counselor to fill in when necessary. That means there will be one more safe place for kids to go. And they'll counsel kids who just *feel* like running away. That will prevent a lot of potential runaways."

"If I'd known where to go for help, I might never have left," Angela admitted. "I was just so confused. . . ."

"And Pastor Lake is helping to set up a hotline

for kids. It's part of a national program, a number to call if you're scared or in trouble. It will also be a way for kids to call home without actually letting anyone know where they are. They can leave messages and pick up messages from their parents. The volunteers who answer will also be trained to talk to kids who are just thinking about running. If the caller has been pushed out of his or her home, then the volunteer will try to put the person in touch with an agency that can find a shelter for them."

"Boy, could I have used that," Angela murmured. "But who's going to pay for this?"

"Well, there's some government funding, and our church is going to help support it. Egg even came up with the idea of singing telegrams! Someone pays us to deliver a song, and the money goes to the hotline. And listen to this! If somebody calls the hotline from a place that doesn't have a shelter, Pastor Lake is going to have a huge list of pastors who will help take care of a runaway in their area."

"So I could have had counseling, a roof over my head, and sent a message to my mom?" Angela said in disbelief. "And I thought I was all alone!"

"You were never alone," Lexi told her. "Not really. We were all praying for you. You had Someone watching over you."

"You're absolutely right," Angela agreed. "Because I didn't get hurt or kidnapped or any of the other things I now realize could have happened to me. I never knew until now how rich I really am."

Lexi gave her a wide grin. "I'm glad you learned quickly. None of us could have taken your being gone much longer."

Chapter Ten

"Mi . . . mi . . . mi. . . ." Binky dramatically warmed up her vocal cords while her brother rolled his eyes. Several of the residents of the mission looked at her with mild interest. They were getting accustomed to seeing the young people around since the runaway hotline concept had been implemented.

"Knock it off," Egg ordered. "You haven't been asked to sing opera, just singing telegrams."

Binky looked unperturbed. "People are *paying* us to do this. That means we have to give them our best. Right, Lexi?"

"I guess," Lexi said reluctantly, not wanting to be dragged into the McNaughtons' continuing debate. "Will says that today will bring in over two hundred dollars."

"That much?" Jennifer was surprised. "Do that many people actually *want* telegrams sung or are they just being nice?"

"We have eleven birthdays, two anniversary parties, a baby shower, a bridal shower, and three just-for-the-fun-of-it telegrams to deliver." Todd read from the list Will had given him.

"Is Mrs. Waverly going with us?" Egg asked, referring to the group's musical advisor. She was very excited about the idea of the Emerald Tones doing the singing telegrams.

"Yes. She should already be here." Lexi frowned. "I wonder where she is?"

"She called to say she might be late. She said something about having a 'wonderful last-minute idea' and having to stop to pick up something." Todd took out a map and began to plot their course for the singing telegram venture.

"I hope she's picking up food," Egg muttered. "A burger would be mighty fine about now. And fries."

"You'd eat up all our profits," Jennifer scolded. "Besides, you'll sing better on an empty stomach."

At that moment, Mrs. Waverly burst into the room, her hair flying haphazardly out of its French twist. She was carrying a large box with the word "Backstage" emblazoned on the sides.

"So sorry to be late, but I had the most marvelous inspiration that I just had to act on. Wait until you see what I brought for you!" She put the box on a nearby table and lifted the lid. Colorful fabrics bloomed out of the box and onto the tabletop. A tiny bell jingled somewhere in the folds.

"What's that?" Binky stared at the brightly hued jumble. "Presents?"

"Costumes!" Mrs. Waverly crowed as she picked

up a huge clown suit in primary colors. "Aren't they wonderful?"

"Sure, but what are they for?" Egg's nose twitched and he stared suspiciously at his teacher.

"This one is for you, I think." Mrs. Waverly held up the costume to Egg's shoulders and studied the effect with a practiced eye. "With some purple hair and a red nose, it will be perfect."

"Pur . . . pur . . . purple?" Egg stammered.

"And, Binky, here's another clown suit that's just your size." Mrs. Waverly whipped out a scarlet contraption that had big fuzzy eyeballs marching down the front like buttons. "Darling, isn't it? Maybe we should have you sing 'I Only Have Eyes For You' while you're wearing this. Wouldn't that be cute?"

Binky stared open-jawed at their teacher.

"You have costumes for all of us?" Jennifer finally managed. "Aren't we wearing our Emerald Tones blazers?"

"There are more clowns, a cowboy or two, a wonderful carrot costume, and a variety of marvelous space aliens. Pick whatever you like."

"Are you sure this is a good idea, Mrs. Waverly?" Lexi asked. "I mean, should we be calling attention to ourselves like this?"

"Of course. We *want* people to know we're doing singing telegrams for the Runaway Hotline fund. What better way than with costumes?"

"What kinds of songs do space aliens sing?" Todd asked. He had put on a mask with a six-fingered hand sprouting out of the top of the head.

"How about 'Row, Row, Row Your Spaceship'?" Jennifer suggested sweetly.

"Mrs. Waverly, we're going to look like fools!" Egg said morosely.

"Just try your hair on. You might like it." Mrs. Waverly thrust a curly purple wig into his hands. Then she fluttered around the room, encouraging everyone to try on a costume.

"It's *you*, Egg!" Jennifer said with a laugh when Egg was dressed. The vertical stripes of the costume made tall, skinny Egg look ten feet tall. The colorful wig was an explosion of bright purple on top of his head.

"You look like a surreal candle," Binky decided as she studied her brother. "With a purple flame."

"You should talk. You look like an M&M."

"Fitting. Sweet and petite. That's me."

Todd had put a drab green gown over his clothing and kept the head with the protruding hand. He was moving around the room, bending over asking everyone to shake it.

Lexi and Jennifer were matching alien princesses in flowing white robes and bald caps. Everyone chose a costume and soon they were all gone.

Mrs. Waverly clapped her hands. "You look wonderful! Todd, where's our first stop?"

Todd stood up, the extra hand flapping in the air. "A birthday party on eighth street. Little kids. Egg, you and Binky had better go in first. My space alien might scare them."

"It scares *me*," Peggy muttered.

The party was already in progress in the back-yard when they arrived. Egg and Binky came around the house first, singing the birthday song. Then Todd explained why they were there and what they were doing. Tiny children and their mothers stared at them as they sang three more songs.

Egg looked down when he felt a tugging on the bottom of his costume. A tiny boy stood there with his arms held out to be picked up.

"Oh, for sweet!" Binky cooed. "Pick him up, Egg."

"I don't think—"

"It's okay," the child's mother said. "He adores clowns."

Egg bent over to pick up the boy. The other children screamed in delight. "More songs, more songs," they chanted.

Willingly the group obliged.

"This is fun!" Binky whispered to Lexi. "I don't mind doing this at all. . . ." Her comment was muf-fled by a shriek from Egg.

Egg suddenly thrust the little boy he was car-rying into his mother's arms. Then he began to pluck at his costume and say, "Yuk. Yuk. Yuk!"

"Did Bobby wet on you? I'm sorry. I should have thought. We're potting training and . . ."

Now everyone was laughing. Except Egg. He was doing a wild clown dance around the yard, flap-ping at the wet spot on his suit. It took Mrs. Waverly to lead him away while the others said good-bye.

After the last telegram was sung, Egg peeled off the dried suit and dropped it in a heap on the mission floor. "We aren't charging enough for this," he said bluntly. "No way."

"Oh, I don't know," Mrs. Waverly said with a smile. She produced an envelope full of cash and checks. "The mother of that little boy gave us twenty extra dollars for the 'little mess.' And everyone tipped us so well that we made nearly three hundred dollars today!"

Egg's expression brightened. "You mean it? Cool." A satisfied expression slid across Egg's face. "Maybe the little kid that sprung a leak wasn't so bad after all!"

———

"I've never done this kind of thing before," Minda said doubtfully. "Can't we just hire someone else to do it?" She was staring at the quilt lying on the floor in the Leightons' living room. "Besides, it's not done yet. What about Angela's block?"

Lexi had asked the girls over to tie the quilt to the batting and backing. Then she would finish the edges and take it to the nursing home in time for the auction sale.

"It will mean more if we do it ourselves. And Angela's block is done. She should be here any minute."

"How did the first day of singing telegrams go?"

Minda asked. "I wish I could have done it first."

"Great! Word is that lots of people are going to use us. They like the idea of the money going to the hotline."

Just then the doorbell rang.

"Hi, it's only me," Angela called. She held her head high, and though she was pale, she was otherwise just the same.

She thrust out her quilt block. "Sorry it's late, but I've been . . . out of town."

It hadn't been easy for Angela to return to school, Lexi knew, but she'd handled it pretty well. By being open, honest, and admitting to her foolishness, she had diffused most of the gossip. Lexi and her other friends had tried to make sure that everyone knew Angela was willing to talk about her experience.

"I'm surprised you didn't bring my brother along," Binky grumbled. "I didn't think he'd leave you alone this long."

"He has been a little overprotective," Angela said with a laugh. "I told him he was suffocating me and that if he didn't want to be stitched to the quilt in place of my block, he'd better lay off for the afternoon."

"Good. You put him in his place. I like that in a woman." Binky grinned slyly.

"Your block! Let's see it," Anna Marie said. "When Lexi sews yours in, our quilt will be whole."

Angela held up the fabric and the girls gasped. It was beautiful. She had embroidered three figures onto the block in different colors of metallic thread. The figures, forming a circle, all held their arms out to one another. In the center was a big red heart, glittering with tiny rhinestone buttons.

"It's my family," Angela stammered. "At least it's the way I see it now. Three people, all reaching out to one another, with a heart in the middle. The heart symbolizes the love we have for each other . . . and for God, who brought me back to them."

Lexi looked up at the sound of a large, unlady-like snuffle. Minda, of all people, was crying!

Now Angela laughed. "And I wish I could do another block, as well. Because I'd do it just the same but with many, many more people on it—one for each of my friends. I realized a lot of things while I was away. I finally figured out how much my mom and Ted love me. And since I've come back, I've realized how much my friends love me, too."

She placed her block into the space they had saved for her. Angela was right. Now everything and everyone felt complete.

A Note From Judy

I'm glad you're reading *Cedar River Daydreams*! I hope I've given you something to think about as well as a story to entertain you. If you feel you have any of the problems that Lexi and her friends experience, I encourage you to talk with your parents, a pastor, or a trusted adult friend. There are many people who care about you!

I love to hear from my readers, so if you'd like to receive my newsletter and a bookmark, please send a self-addressed, stamped envelope to:

Judy Baer
Bethany House Publishers
11300 Hampshire Avenue South
Minneapolis, MN 55438

———

Be sure to watch for my *Dear Judy . . .* books at your local bookstore. These books are full of questions that you, my readers, have asked in your letters, along with my response. Just about every topic is covered—from dating and romance to friendships and parents. Hope to hear from you soon!

Dear Judy, What's It Like at Your House?
Dear Judy, Did You Ever Like a Boy
    (who didn't like you?)

Live! From Brentwood High

1 ▪ Risky Assignment
2 ▪ Price of Silence
3 ▪ Double Danger
4 ▪ Sarah's Dilemma
5 ▪ Undercover Artists
6 ▪ Faded Dreams

Other Books by Judy Baer

▪ Dear Judy, What's It Like at Your House?
▪ Dear Judy, Did You Ever Like a Boy
  (who didn't like you?)
▪ Paige
▪ Pamela

Teen Series From
Bethany House Publishers

Early Teen Fiction (11–14)

HIGH HURDLES by Lauraine Snelling
Show jumper DJ Randall strives to defy the odds and achieve her dream of winning Olympic Gold.

SUMMERHILL SECRETS by Beverly Lewis
Fun-loving Merry Hanson encounters mystery and excitement in Pennsylvania's Amish country.

THE TIME NAVIGATORS by Gilbert Morris
Travel back in time with Danny and Dixie as they explore unforgettable moments in history.

Young Adult Fiction (12 and up)

CEDAR RIVER DAYDREAMS by Judy Baer
Experience the challenges and excitement of high school life with Lexi Leighton and her friends—over one million books sold!

GOLDEN FILLY SERIES by Lauraine Snelling
Readers are in for an exhilarating ride as Tricia Evanston races to become the first female jockey to win the sought-after Triple Crown.

JENNIE MCGRADY MYSTERIES by Patricia Rushford
A contemporary Nancy Drew, Jennie McGrady's sleuthing talents promise to keep readers on the edge of their seats.

LIVE! FROM BRENTWOOD HIGH by Judy Baer
When eight teenagers invade the newsroom, the result is an action-packed teen-run news show exploring the love, laughter, and tears of high school life.

THE SPECTRUM CHRONICLES by Thomas Locke
Adventure and romance await readers in this fantasy series set in another place and time.

SPRINGSONG BOOKS by various authors
Compelling love stories and contemporary themes promise to capture the hearts of readers.

WHITE DOVE ROMANCES by Yvonne Lehman
Romance, suspense, and fast-paced action for teens committed to finding pure love.